MIL
Miller, Calvin.
Shade /

AMES PUBLIC LIBRARY
AMES, IOWA

WITHDRAWN

X

3

Shade

Calvin Miller

Shade

A NOVEL

BETHANYHOUSE
PUBLISHERS
MINNEAPOLIS, MINNESOTA

564044

Shade
Copyright © 2001
Calvin Miller

Cover art: *Farm By A Lake* © Vincent McIndoe/SIS
Cover design by Dan Thornberg

All rights reserved. No part of this publication may be reproduced,
stored in a retrieval system, or transmitted in any form or by any
means—electronic, mechanical, photocopying, recording, or
otherwise—without the prior written permission of the publisher
and copyright owners.

Published by Bethany House Publishers
A Ministry of Bethany Fellowship International
11400 Hampshire Avenue South
Bloomington, Minnesota 55438
www.bethanyhouse.com

Printed in the United States of America

Library of Congress Cataloging-in-Publication Data

Miller, Calvin.
   Shade / by Calvin Miller.
      p. cm.
Sequel to: Wind.
   ISBN 0-7642-2363-1   (alk. paper)
   1. King of Prussia (Pa.)—Fiction. I. Title.
   PS3563.I376   S48   2001
   813'.54—dc21

                                                      2001003782

As with snow and wind,

so with shade,

to Melanie

CALVIN MILLER is a poet, a pastor, a theologian, a painter, and one of Christianity's best-loved writers with over thirty published books. His writing spans a wide spectrum of genres, from the bestselling SINGER TRILOGY to *The Unchained Soul* to the heart-rending novellas *Snow* and *Wind*. Miller presently serves as professor of preaching and pastoral ministries at Beeson Divinity School in Alabama, where he and his wife, Barbara, make their home.

A bronze sundial and a steel mailbox fried the bright air above them. The sundial was in the Muellers' yard, the mailbox in the McCaslins'.

A sparrow landed briefly on the bronze stylus of the sundial, then promptly fluttered into the fern bed. The sparrow's short visit to the sizzling metal made it clear the sundial was very hot. But it wasn't the dial that was hot, it was the June sun. Ingrid didn't need a thermometer to tell her it was hot. It was only three weeks until the summer solstice, when the heat would stretch as endlessly as the days.

Looking out the window, Ingrid could see that the shadow of the stylus fell across the bronze plate of the dial, landing its dark wedge of a shadow across the Roman numeral one, which told her it was time to give Hans the medicine for his hurting back. She usually used the clock to schedule his doses, but this time the sundial would work just as well.

9

"It's time for your medicine, Hans," she said.

"Vhat makes you think so?" said Hans, grimacing in pain as he adjusted himself on the couch.

"I can see it on the face of the sundial."

"Is the clock broke?" he asked, grinning.

"No, but the clock agrees with the sundial."

"All right then. But if you don't mind, I'd rather take my medicine using the clock than the dial."

"Well, the sun never lies," Ingrid said indifferently. "Besides, the sundial not only tells the right time, it tells the temperature too."

"How so?" asked Hans.

"When the little birds land but don't stay long on the bronze dial."

"Vhen der little birdies burn their little feet it's hot, is that it?"

"I just saw a sparrow land and leave the dial in a quick flit."

Hans rolled his eyes and took his medicine. Ingrid returned to the window. The old sundial had been in their family for years. Around the face of the green bronze dial was a quote from the Ninetieth Psalm that read, "Teach us to number our days."

Just thinking of the Psalm made Ingrid shudder as she looked at Hans and turned quickly away. He was scheduled to have a biopsy on Monday. This idea caused her to shudder a second time. She turned away from the chill she felt—a chill in the middle of the hottest June day she had ever known. Life was a mishmash of fire and ice. The fire was the sun on her garden dial; the ice was a dread of which she could not speak.

Ingrid returned to the world at hand and knew somehow it would be a long and hot summer. June was usually a spring month, but the sun was already too beastly to let the spring go on any longer. *Two months of spring means four months of summer,* she told herself. *It's enough to boil a sinless soul in purgatory....* Then she remembered she was a Lutheran who had no need of such notions.

❧

"Keep your bonnet on. No need to fry your mind," Peter shouted to Isabel as she left the house and headed for the mailbox. The sun seemed to have a grudge against eastern Pennsylvania, determined to burn some bright respect into the state. Isabel snugged her bonnet laces underneath her chin, stepped from beneath the shade of the wide eaves of her home, and hurried into the sunlight.

In spite of the heat, Isabel McCaslin "had her head about her," as the Amish would have put it. She was a settled woman in every sense of the word. She had taken a stand against hard times by offering each new day her incorrigible generosity. She wasn't apt to spend a penny on herself but had remained generous to all who were in need.

Her radical, religious crazy days were over. Her view of her hometown was now sadder but wiser. For she'd come to understand that not everyone who talked about God in church acted much like Him once they left worship. She did believe that wherever God existed, He could be found in abundance. However, Isabel generally felt God was easier to locate at small, honest altars than in showy churches.

She would sometimes see an Amish couple riding along in their horse-drawn buggy and envy them for their simplicity. Not that she admired their aloof lifestyle. One cannot be committed to black hats and bonnets without making God look disinterested in the world at hand. They dressed in black and saw God as white. But black and white were as honest and self-proclaiming as a checkerboard. Black and white had much to commend them in so many churches where gray was the color of boredom. Gray was a cowardly color to Isabel McCaslin.

While helping the Pitovskys through their ordeal of tuberculosis and healing, she'd managed to keep Ernest Pitovsky on the payroll at the dairy farm. Of course, Peter had resented her hiring Ernest yet was prevented from firing him because of a photograph Isabel kept in a sealed envelope in her safe-deposit box at the bank. It was a shocking picture of Isabel, taken just after Peter had roughed her up during one of his temper tantrums. True, it was a kind of blackmail, and although Isabel didn't much like using such a method to get her way, she could think of no other course of action at the time to hold her brother at bay. It didn't seem Christian to blackmail

Peter into behaving like a Christian. But what's a sister to do with a brother who had been acting so unbrotherly? No, she was doing the right thing. Mean Christians must sometimes be dealt with in ways that keep them from injuring others.

All in all, Isabel was living in a gentle agreement with the rest of her world as she walked to the mailbox the first Monday in June. "Oww!" she cried as she reached and touched the hot lid of the steel mailbox. It had been brought to near foundry temperatures by the sun, making the air inside the box feel like a blast furnace.

Isabel was amazed to see only one letter in the box. Usually there were at least two or three pieces of mail related to her brother, Peter, and the dairy farm: bills from creditors, or checks from customers whose payments kept the farm up and running. The mail was rarely addressed to her. But on this sun-bleached day the only piece of mail was hers.

She looked at the letter and grimaced, for she instantly recognized the handwriting on the envelope. She'd received many letters written in this hand during one long-gone era of her life. During those days, she believed she was in love with the man who had penned her an entire collection of letters. She looked to be sure that no one was looking, then untucked and used the tail of her shirt as a potholder to snap the fiery metal lid of the mailbox shut.

Isabel tucked her shirt back into her skirt, then

13

stood for a moment in the blistery sunlight and studied the letter. She held it at first at some distance as if afraid. This wasn't a letter to be opened immediately, so she stuck it into the pocket of her cotton skirt and started toward the house. The odd letter was about as hot as the mailbox that had held it. It seemed to burn her flesh even through her skirt, and just the thought of the sender brought back a flood of old memories.

Four years earlier she had fallen head over heels in love. Her love had been a passionate offering of soul to one not worth it. For most there is no restraint in the giving of first love. Isabel had fallen hard and had given Cupid her full allegiance, believing first loves are less than real unless openly displayed. True love should enjoy its euphoria, be capricious and showy.

But now this letter was unwelcome.

Again she was in love ... love! A mature love it was too! *Otto,* she thought, *I love you.* She felt the letter and frowned over her naïve younger days, her spurious, immature, long-ago notions of love. She felt a hot trickle of perspiration roll down her face as the Pennsylvania sun dislodged her reminiscences. She was back in the hot world at hand. All things back then were back then. Now was now. And between the *thens* and the *nows* were four years, most of which she had waited for a letter—indeed she had counted on a letter to keep her soul alive.

"Good grief, sun, back off!" she muttered. She

quickened her steps to the shade of the great elm at the edge of the drive. *Shade, I bless you. The world is a griddle in your absence,* she thought. She took the letter from her pocket and leaned back against the thick trunk of the tree to study it.

This letter four years earlier would have delighted her. But times were different now—hard and different. There was Otto, all that she could hope for in a man. He was kind, thoughtful, poetic. It seemed to her that in many ways Otto needed her. They had declared their love for each other. They sat together in church and walked all over town hand in hand. There was an expectation throughout the community that they were a committed couple who would soon be making an announcement about their future together. The idea of being married to Otto was altogether fulfilling to Isabel.

She stepped into the hot light and hurried toward the next set of cool shadows.

The shady eaves of the house welcomed her back from the long scorching trip to the mailbox.

Once back in the house, she passed her sister-in-law, Kathleen, who was nursing her baby, Elizabeth. Isabel smiled but said nothing. She continued on to her room and sat down on her bed. She looked at the letter again. *Should I open it or tear it into little pieces?* she wondered. *No, I must read it, but read it fast. But what if it's too foreboding? I must make no sudden moves here.*

She laid the letter on the small desk in her room

and walked back out through the living room and into the kitchen and leisurely made herself a pot of tea. She found a lemon and sliced it, then pulled from the cupboard a heavy mug. *What else do I need? Five lumps of sugar. Usually three would be enough, but I may need the extra energy to deal with this.* Setting everything on a tray, she made her way back to her room.

I have to make myself read this letter, she said to herself, picking it up. Then she whispered, "Oh, Otto, may there be no barriers to our newfound love." She opened the letter and began to read.

> *Dear Izzy, I realize it has been far too long since I've written. . . .*

"Four years, you crumb!" she interjected. "Yes, that's far too long!"

> *But my little chickie Bible baby, I have seen the error of my folly. . . .*

"How odd, and how corny! You four-flushing cad." Isabel remembered how he always used to call her his little chickie Bible baby. She wondered why—even at twenty-two years of age—she had ever thought the phrase reasonable or cute.

> *I'm coming back to King of Prussia and you will find me much different. When you last knew me, I was just a Bible salesman, but now I truly love the Word of God. I read it just like you do. I am ashamed of what I once was. I once milked*

that little town like you milked your cows. I took from it and gave nothing back. That was how I handled all of life. I was a taker, not a giver. Then one day I was reading the epistle of Peter, where he was talking about the Second Coming, you know, where Peter says the Day of the Lord will come like a thief in the night, when the elements will melt with a fervent heat and the earth and everything in it will be burned up.

Well, my dearest chickie, trust me when I say that it was not that part of the verse that most spoke to me. It was the part where Peter asks the question, "Seeing then that all these things shall be dissolved, what manner of persons ought ye to be?" Suddenly I saw what kind of person I had become, and I knew how much I had disappointed you, the only true love I've ever known. So 2 Peter 3:11 has turned my whole life around. The apostle's question has haunted me. Jesus is coming again and the world is going to be burned up. What sort of man should I be then, Izzy? Oh, my dearest, dearest chickie Bible baby, what sort of man should I be? I was so selfish in the past, but now I'm into Jesus, truly into Jesus. I've become a minister! I work in the center of Philadelphia, helping Sister Zella distribute food to gutter bums.

"How appropriate! A bum helping other bums! You snake, you had better flee before the wrath to come!" Isabel seethed with anger and disbelief.

Of course, I still sell Bibles. But the moment I truly gave my life back to God, I instantly saw I could no longer sell the World-Hope Family Bible *as I once did. It was not a good product, and Jesus helped me see that. He helped me to see that in merely selling a very bad Good Book, I had been acting unethically with the Word of God. So immediately I repented of my folly and began selling the* Three Generation Regal Heritage Bible. *It has a much better binding and a thumb index, so I feel like people are truly getting a better deal. Only I don't think of it as making deals. That's all in my past. I think of it as spreading light and truth, for just three easy payments of $3.33 each. People all over are being changed by God's Word, brought to them by a man who has been changed by God's Word.*

So, Izzy, I beg you to forgive me. You are the one true love I've ever known. I need your forgiveness. I plan to arrive in King of Prussia next week. I want to see you first thing. I will sell no Bibles until I know you have forgiven me, or at least not very many. Even then, I will only sell what I need to continue my ministry to the bums. Am I not changed? I won't sign my name as I once did, as Benny the Bible Guy. I am a new man and so I sign it just as Benjamin Baxter, God is my King! Bibles are my thing!

Isabel McCaslin didn't want to hear that Benny was coming back to King of Prussia. His abandonment of her love was an extinguisher that had snuffed the smoldering end of her adolescence. She wanted nothing more to do with him. She looked at the small empty pewter frame that once held his picture. But her love for Otto had caused her to remove Benny's picture from the frame and stuff it in the bottom of a drawer. She wasn't sure that Benny—or Benjamin—had changed, but she was quite sure that *she* had. She had no intention of ever letting him back into her life.

She finished her tea and returned the tray to the kitchen. *I will never forgive you for what you did to me, Benny—I mean, Benjamin. "How oft shall my brother sin against me, and I forgive him? till seven times?" No, unfortunately, the Scriptures say, "Until seventy times seven."* That added up to 490 times. While the number was excessive, she wasn't sure if she had forgiven him quite that many times. Still, he had been the first love of her life. He was right about milking the town for profit. But while he'd milked the community for all it was worth, he had been reasonably good to her. Then she remembered his athletic build, his square chin, trim waist, and barrel chest. Like the lover in the Song of Songs, he had teeth like a flock of sheep just shorn, coming up from the washing. Each had its twin and not one of them was alone. Isabel smiled as she recalled the happy times. His reputation as a shyster gradually dissolved into the better parts of his personality. She remembered how she had first felt about him. He was as enthralling as a carnival barker, and she was the young girl struck by the glitz of the midway—a thousand

twirling lights and the angled perimeter of a spinning Ferris wheel.

*Thy love was fair to me, my brother, as a stag bounding
across the hills, as a merchant of goodly ships. Otto, stay
with me. Don't leave me, Otto.* But try as she might,
Otto became swallowed up in old vapors.

The former images flooded back into Isabel's
consciousness, though the images were not wholly
welcome. They came dressed in a lost melancholy
and the madness of a fascination she thought had
left for good. She suddenly felt needy, as if losing
her grip on things. Her old skewed way of seeing the
world fell back upon her, entering her mind like an
unwelcome guest who plans to stay for a long visit.

While she experienced this disconcerting sensation, she didn't realize she was now thinking much
as she used to think. She thought about Benny
nearly every time she read the Bible he had given
her. Benny had taught her to love the Bible and now
he was coming back ... after all these years. What
should she do? He was a shyster, wasn't he? But
what if he had really changed? What if God really
was his King? What if the Bible really was his thing?
Who was she to be harsh to a man who had apparently seen the error of his former ways, especially if
he was truly sorry that he'd broken her heart? Do
not honest prodigals need their hope restored?

There was no sorting through her questions all
at once. Also, there was Otto.

Otto had loved her when she needed him, and

yet he hadn't seen her as needy. Otto had seen her as complete until she became exactly what he saw her to be. Otto saw her as well, and his vision helped to heal her. Could she ever take his love and cast it away? She thought of using a method that Benny had taught her to determine the will of God. She felt a little childish considering the old method of a shyster Bible salesman. But now there was a new Benny. Maybe it would actually work.

Isabel opened her Bible, closed her eyes, and prayed, *God, speak to me from thy Word. Thy Word is a lamp to my feet and a light to my path. I will trust in thee.* She put her finger down firmly on the unseen page, her eyes still clamped shut. She was aware she'd opened the Bible somewhere near the end of it, to give Otto the edge in the matter, she figured. She felt the Song of Solomon or some of the middle books of the Bible would be friendlier to Benny, whereas Revelation at the end would be sure to be more friendly to Otto. Isabel opened her eyes and read, " 'Nevertheless I have somewhat against thee, because thou hast left thy first love. Remember therefore from whence thou art fallen, and repent.' Revelation two, verses four and five."

Benny was her first love!

It was a sign!

Benny was coming again.

So was Jesus, though somehow she believed Benny would be arriving first.

I'm afraid it's cancer," said Dr. Drummond. There it was, spoken too suddenly—a whole slate of bad news in a single utterance. Ingrid blinked and tried to erase reality. The kind practitioner seemed instantly unkind. The surgery waiting room was blasted with icy air.

"I'm sorry, Ingrid," the doctor said. "Terribly sorry."

Ingrid felt there was something good in knowing how bad the bad news was. The demon of fear that had been sitting beside Ingrid as she had waited for the test results was now exorcised. She knew that hearing the worst could somehow keep a person from fearing it. Yet, even after she'd heard the results, she wished she hadn't. Now she wanted to reverse everything, remain in a state of hopeful waiting.

She stared straight ahead as if searching for an answer on the blank wall behind Dr. Drummond. Was this the same amiable family doctor who had always healed their family, who had cared for her boys throughout their childhood? Where had that doctor gone? And what had happened to the comfortable, familiar world of eastern Pennsylvania, her home where she'd always known such happiness?

Suddenly there wasn't enough air in the room. She gasped after it, but her lungs remained unsatisfied, her tongue unmovable in her mouth. How could Dr. Drummond say the horrible thing he'd just said?

But there it was. Hard words often come fast, and the speed at which they come breaks the heart with their casual desperation.

Ingrid hesitated, waiting for her mind to catch up with what she'd just heard. She hoped Dr. Drummond would burst out into laughter and say "Gotcha!" or "April fools!" But the physician said nothing, nothing at all.

After what seemed an eternity of silence, he did finally speak. "I'm terribly sorry, Mrs. Mueller," he repeated.

Don't call me "Mrs. Mueller"! I'm Ingrid. We're friends, she thought. Ingrid then found the breath to ask, "But it can be taken out and then Hans will be all right?"

"It's inoperable," flew his words. "The cancer is too far advanced. If we had caught it earlier . . . but it now has metastasized from his back area to all through his lower abdomen and upper torso. I'm afraid the cancer's gone too far to fix, Ingrid."

Metastasized was one of those big words that doctors used so that patients would have to set aside their shock while they tried to define it. Medicine had its own lectionary, its book of word games and scientific terms. Ingrid turned the word over and over in her mind until at last it did define itself. The ugly word fell like a stone on the numbness of her soul.

Then her shock gave way to impropriety. She collapsed against her longtime friend and physician and held to him, he being the only fixed object in the spinning room. Tears poured forth from her eyes, which helped to lessen the stinging in her brain. The doctor's encircling arms held her close as if to fortify her for the job that lay ahead. Ingrid knew what she had to do. She would have to tell Hans the terrible news. But *how* was she to tell him? Hans would want to know all at once the things she'd wanted to know all at once. He would want to know if anything could be done, if there should be a second opinion. He would want to know how long he had to live.

Ingrid couldn't understand why Dr. Drummond had told the bad news to her first. Why hadn't he told both of them at the same time? But she knew the answer. Hans was caught up in the half world that lay between ether-induced consciousness and engulfing agony. Only in the kindness of a morphine stupor would he be able to sleep above the screaming pain of his sutures. So Ingrid had to be the first to know. It is a burden to bear bad news and a greater burden to carry it inside until it can be passed on. She shuddered. The ugly work was hers. She would have to tell Hans.

"How much ..." But Ingrid couldn't finish the obvious question.

"Not much longer," said Dr. Drummond, graciously supplying what he knew she was asking. "It could be as little as a month ... perhaps as long as three or four months. No more, Ingrid."

Ingrid said nothing else. It was clear that their thirty-five years of marriage were spiraling downward into an abyss, and the velocity of the plunge was out of control.

"Do you want me to tell him, when he comes around?"

"Would you please? I'll be there, but would you please tell him the minute he's fully aware again? He'll want to know more than I can tell him."

"Of course," the doctor agreed. "That should be sometime tomorrow morning. Shall we meet here around nine, then?"

Ingrid nodded.

Then with a final embrace, Dr. Drummond turned and left the room.

Ingrid settled down into the too-soft cushions of the large chair. At the moment she hadn't the inclination to see her beloved Hans. Instead, she allowed herself to doze for a while, hoping she might drift off and awake later to some happier reality. Then all at once she was roused by the arrival of her two sons. A brightness suffused the room as they entered.

"How's Papa?" Erick asked.

Ingrid rose from the chair, went over and hugged her younger son, and began sobbing. He was far slighter than Dr. Drummond, yet his thin chest and angular arms gathered his mother into a tight embrace. Otto opened his arms and joined them, and soon they were all crying. They knew the awful truth before Ingrid could speak it.

For most of the past year Hans Mueller had been suffering and had spent most of his time in bed because of the intense pain in his back. Both his family and the entire community thought it only a pulled muscle or perhaps a slipped disk. No one had suspected this most recent diagnosis by Dr. Drummond. Hans was much sicker than they'd all thought.

The family coal business had been suffering as well. Ingrid discovered that the mildness of the late winter had proved harder on their savings than any of them imagined. Whatever treatment and medicines Hans's illness required would about use up what little money they'd struggled to save during the warmer than usual spring. To make matters worse, Hans had purchased and stored extra coal the fall before, fearing the strike in Appalachia would result in their not having enough coal on hand should the winter turn out to be severe. But the strike and the weather had not transpired in the way Hans predicted. Now they found that he'd invested a great deal of money in buying coal that still remained unsold.

Erick guessed what Ingrid was thinking. "Mama, you know the extra money I've been saving from my teaching wages is yours if you should need it. All of it. I have seven hundred dollars that survived the bank closure last fall."

"Erick, I couldn't ask you to do that. You and Mary and Alexis will . . ."

Erick's wire-rimmed spectacles traveled up his nose as he scowled at her, indicating there would be no arguing about it. "If we do marry, it won't be before late fall, and Mary has a house we can live in till you and Papa get things stabilized."

Otto, who had been sitting quietly the whole time, suddenly spoke up. "Mama, I don't have any money saved. In fact, I've used too much of yours and Papa's resources already. But this I promise you—I'll keep the coal business going. I won't be able to sell much in July, but soon I can begin preselling the coal for next winter, plus I'll see if I can sell to a few of the city generators in Philadelphia. I don't need to remind either of you how much I owe you for helping me with Marguerite."

Otto's child was the gift of Easter and a miracle of the east wind. Ingrid had been thrilled when two months earlier Marguerite had come into their lives. Hans was crazy about her, for she delighted in listening to his many tales of life in the old country when he was a boy. Hans had told her of the snow in Bavaria and how far they had to walk to get to school. And he wasn't above exaggerating the details.

"But, Otto," Erick said, "what if you and Isabel should—"

"Whoa! Let's don't speed things along so fast," Otto said, interrupting Erick's inference with eye-level resistance. "We have had some great talks and one or two special moments on my coal deliveries. . . ."

"And don't forget the peaches and cream on the porch swing," chided Erick.

"Whoa, Erick. Peaches and cream on a porch swing does not an engagement make." Otto was holding his hand up like a New York police officer. "I'm not sure Isabel is ready for instant motherhood."

"Well, Marguerite and Isabel look to be pretty good friends in church."

"Both of you boys seem to be destined be to fathers and husbands at the same time." Ingrid laughed, then appeared as though she felt guilty for making fun. "Hans," she said soberly.

Reality had returned.

What right did she have to be talking and laughing as if nothing at all was wrong. Everything was wrong. They were standing in the waiting room of a Philadelphia hospital. The normal world they

loved—the world where they spoke of family, wed-
dings, and the future—was now light-years away in
the bright land of King of Prussia. They must soon
go back there to get on with living . . . and dying.

"The doctor said Hans would be under sedation
until morning," Ingrid said. "So let's go home and
come back tomorrow first thing."

She gathered up her satchel that contained a ball
of yarn and two ivory-spiked knitting needles and
then grabbed her purse. And with a son on either
side of her, the wounded trio headed toward the
door. The hospital's narrow corridor barely accom-
modated them as they moved through it. The even
narrower turnstile of the revolving door forced the
three of them to split into single passengers. Ingrid
hated even the momentary inconvenience. The spinning door was a reminder that some of life's pas-
sages must be taken alone. She stumbled forward
into the revolving glass, and the door turned her out
into a world that felt evil and hostile, into streets
full of strange forms.

Hans and Ingrid were not one word after all. For
years Ingrid had thought of their names as a four-
syllable phrase spoken all together and at once. Yet
now the unthinkable was upon them. *Hans and
Ingrid* was a word soon to be hacked apart. They had
spoken all their lives about which of them would be
the first to . . .

Ingrid broke into tears.

Hans would die soon. She was alone. Although

Ingrid had her family, she knew that when Hans left her, her grief would be too great for her to stay buoyed up by the knowledge that, in their younger years, they had raised two boys together.

She sensed the world was spinning again. As she felt herself start to fall backward toward the sidewalk, Erick and Otto, who were stepping through the revolving door behind her, saw her sinking and, in a single swift action, pushed through the door and caught their mother, one on each side, before she dropped to the pavement.

Ingrid's two sons were off to their separate oracles. Erick arrived at Mary's and bid her to sit down to tell her the awful news.

"But, Erick, darling, can nothing be done?"

"No, Mary... nothing."

They both sat in silence as though examining the truth more closely might change it into something more palatable.

"Mary, you've come to be for the Muellers a boulder emerging in our uncertain seas."

"Erick, your brother's poetic spirit sometimes comes alive in you. You credit me with more strength than I contain."

"Not at all."

Alexis, who had been sitting quietly, suddenly bolted into the center of their conversation. "Mama, is Grandpa Hans sick?"

"Yes, Alexis... very sick."

"Does he have asthma?" Mary could see it was a natural assumption for Alexis. She'd been so sick

31

with asthma that it had become the greatest concern in their family. She presumed that all serious sickness was like her sickness.

"No, Alexis, but he's very sick."

"Do we need to pray for him?"

"That is just what he needs," Erick interjected. "Grandpa Hans would be glad to know that you are praying for him."

❧

Erick stayed long after Alexis had gone to bed.

He and Mary sat together in the quiet living room. "Mary, darling, I hope Papa lives to see us married. He's so fond of you."

Mary could tell what Erick's next words would be.

"Do you think we could marry earlier in the fall than we had planned?" he asked.

"Well," Mary replied, "I see no great reason not to. We *are* fixed on the occasion and on our love. The calendar should serve Hans as well as ourselves."

Erick kissed her. Then again. Mary was slumped in the cushions of the couch, and Erick edged even closer. Then he kissed her more ardently than she felt comfortable with.

"Hey, Casanova, let's cool down a bit." Mary sat up straight and pushed Erick upward into a more vertical posture as well. "We started out with the kiss of sound counsel. It was nice and everything, but now you're moving pretty quickly toward something else," she laughed.

"I can take a hint," Erick said.

"Good! Maybe you oughta take it home with you. Come back when you get back in charge of yourself."

Erick grinned. "Just trying to be friendly."

"Get any friendlier and I'll have to call the constable."

They both smiled as they stood.

"Mary, could you stop and see Papa in a day or so, after he gets home?"

She nodded.

"Take Alexis with you. Maybe one night after school."

"Of course."

Erick moved forward to kiss Mary on the lips, but she leaned back and extended her hand instead. He growled and pretended to bite it. Then they parted.

❦

As soon as Otto left his mother to her agonizing evening of dealing with life in all its finality, he went to make a call on Isabel. With all he had to say, the dairy seemed far away. The ten minutes of heavy thinking slowed the old truck he drove to the heavy business of telling the hard truth at the journey's end. He knew she would want to know all the details of Hans's diagnosis. But he found her in the oddest of moods. She was remote, as if only her body were in Pennsylvania. Her mind was on vacation in some distant world, though he knew not exactly how distant.

"Papa will die soon," he told Isabel. "There is nothing more to be done, the doctors say. It's going to be hard on us all, on Mama especially. Isabel, I think that all of us are going to have to hang together to be sure that Mama makes it through this." Tears were swimming in Otto's eyes now. But, surprisingly, there were no tears in Isabel's. She was almost indifferent to Otto's reaching out to her.

" 'It is appointed unto men once to die . . .' " Her voice trailed off, then she returned long enough to say, "It's in Hebrews."

"It's also a very cold response," Otto said.

"Maybe, but it's from the Word, and the Word of God cannot be broken."

Otto was confused. The recently healed Isabel had left town and the old one was back. She was spouting Scripture again, using the Bible in a twisted way in an attempt to avoid reality. Something evil had called her old craziness back to life. She was behaving in the same fanatic manner that once had the community calling her "Dizzy Izzy." But why? Otto couldn't say.

"Isabel! Why are you acting this way? Where have you gone?"

" 'Ye shall seek me, and find me, when ye shall search for me with all your heart.' "

Otto took her by the shoulders and held her gaze with his own bewildered eyes. "Where are you, my darling?"

She stared at him blankly.

"I need you. Please, Isabel, don't do this!" Otto pleaded.

"Let me first bid good-bye to the other maidens," she said.

Otto knew it was the statement of Jephthah's daughter, though he recognized the words more from the opera than from the Bible.

He held her again, forcing her eyes into his. Their vision met but not the minds behind it. She was somewhere else, wild and absent, like she'd been when Otto first met her, only worse. Her eyes were so vacant that Otto's filled with fresh tears. There was nothing else to say; nothing could bring her back. He kissed her on the cheek, but she drew back. He hugged her yet her resolution was firm, her body stiff. "Isabel, please come back." Then Otto turned slowly toward the door. She didn't follow him.

Otto had heard of her previous affliction. Those who were kind spoke of the old Isabel as once being mentally ill. The unkind said she was just a religious nut. All said her condition had been triggered by her losses in love. Her long-ago Bible salesman had left town, taking her mind with him. But now the old Isabel, the old *Izzy*, was back. Suddenly Otto felt guilty thinking of her as Izzy.

Otto wondered whether the community would

understand his willingness to wait on her to get better. He knew the gossipy heart of the townsfolk. He
knew that they'd never called her just Izzy. It was
always "Dizzy Izzy." The name tightened his throat
even though he couldn't, wouldn't, say it out loud.
He turned on the porch, begging in a hurried second of prayer that God would give her back to him
as she had been only days before.

But he counted too much on this fast, desperate
prayer. Isabel stood frozen of mind and frame, like
the pale statue in *The Winter's Tale*. Otto was moved
to utter despair. Still, he couldn't help studying
Isabel as he backed off her front porch.

He looked at her one last time framed in the
doorway. The incandescent lights from the house
made her hair appear flaxen. He couldn't imagine
what inner fiend, in but a single day, had stolen his
beloved. What had summoned this lifeless, Scrip-
ture-spouting demon back into the body so recently
healed? He could find no answer.

He hurried home and went to his room without
mentioning the odd occurrence to Ingrid. She had
enough to worry about without immediately con-
cerning herself with Isabel. But Otto's furious love
spent itself by staring up at the small chandelier in
his bedroom. Only after a long time did he sit down
at the little writing table and take up his pen.

My love has left the planet of all reason.
Where has she gone?

I must pursue her—catch her lost awareness,
Beg her straying soul return.
Come back to me.
One mind can do the work of two,
One heart pump love enough for all.
Cross the shallow sea of lost remembrance.
To the thinner shores of our lost longing.

Otto wrote no more. His lamentation grew silent, though it still remained locked inside him and continued to groan. He feared the night and dreaded the morning.

❧

Across town Kathleen told Isabel's brother, Peter, "Izzy's back!"

"Izzy?" he said.

"I'm afraid so. She seems as sick as ever."

Peter shook his head.

"And one other thing!"

"Yes."

"So is Benny. At least he will be soon." She showed Peter the letter Benny had sent to Isabel. "And, Peter," Kathleen said, "the old pewter frame that was empty while Isabel had her wits about her is filled once again with Benny's old picture. Benny the Bible Guy is coming back."

Peter knew as did Kathleen it might as well have been a picture of Lucifer. His pervasive evil could take a strong young woman from King of Prussia and maroon her on the far side of her mind. Isabel was alone, and her soul would admit no visitors.

She's got too much makeup on, thought Benjamin Baxter. He studied the woman seated directly across from him. They were nearly touching knees as the old train rattled and banged its way along the tracks. "The sun sure is hot today," Benjamin said. "There must be quite a summer on the way. Know what I think, Miss?" She looked distracted, not even nodding a reply. Unaffected by her refusal to acknowledge his conversation, Benjamin went on. "I think sometimes God gets to napping and lets the sun drift far too close to the earth. Then the cornfields dry up and old people get strokes. Any year we have a mild summer, it's 'cause God stays awake and keeps his confounded sun at a safe distance."

Benjamin's attempt to draw the woman into conversation had failed. She smiled and turned abruptly toward the grimy glass of the railcar's window.

That's good, Benjamin told himself. *I'll look out the*

38

window too. She certainly is a hard-looking customer. He guessed her age to be thirty-five or forty, though it could be she was older, given the way she looked. Benjamin might have used the same words to apply to himself. But, of course, he thought too much of Benjamin to think of himself so meanly.

It was a good day for looking out windows, that is, had there been good windows to look through. Alas, they were streaked with railroad soot. The two strangers might have gone on for quite a distance not talking to each other, except that shortly after his comment on the weather, the woman's hefty carpetbag jostled off the chrome luggage rack above them and fell onto Benjamin's lap. The bag was heavy—probably filled with canned goods. Times were hard, and so canned food became like gold after the money dried up. Because of what had happened on Wall Street, people took to buying groceries like they once bought stocks. A lot of these people carried their pantry with them these days. Benny himself always kept a few cans of sardines and Vienna sausages in his valise. This well-painted matron was smuggling her own little bit of life into Pennsylvania with her. Benjamin thought of the small cache in his own satchel and smiled at her.

Still, the plop of what felt like a fifty-pound bag onto his lap had instantly drawn Benjamin's attention from the Pennsylvania countryside to what now lay across his legs.

"Oww!" he'd cried, more startled than hurt by the falling object.

There was no need to ask to whom the bag belonged. No sooner had he yelped than the woman opposite him lunged forward and grabbed the bag. She then attempted to put it back on the luggage rack above them, but it was just too heavy. Benjamin jumped up to help her. With both of them struggling at it, they were able to lift the bag back into its spot on the rack.

"I'm sorry," she said in a way that left Benjamin Baxter in doubt as to whether or not she really was.

"Whew! That's some tonnage in that bag," he said. "You smuggling steel into the state?"

She looked away from him again. Now it became a kind of irresistible game for him. He was convinced that they'd probably never be friends, but now more than ever he was determined to get her to say something.

Benjamin smiled. "On second thought, let me guess. You sell anvils?"

She didn't.

She turned her head to look back out through the dirty glass.

Benjamin smiled again, deciding to continue playing the game:

"Oh, my girl's a dentist up in Duluth.
She'll fill your mouth with pig iron;
She's pig-iron Ruth."

The woman, who longed to be left alone, was in no mood to join his nonsense. Nevertheless, she turned to him and thanked him. "It was nice of you to help me get my bag back up on the shelf."

"Who helped you get it onto the train?"

"The conductor," she replied curtly.

"The strongest men work on these trains," laughed Benjamin.

He laughed alone. She went immediately back to looking out the coach window.

"Don't you want to know where I'm from?" he asked.

She didn't.

"Say, haven't we met before? Yes, that's it! We've met before—I never forget a face. Of course, that monogram on your handkerchief, a C. It stands for Cartwright, doesn't it?" She looked surprised. He had actually guessed at her name and gotten it right. He was all prepared to guess Carson next, or Campbell, but it was clear he'd gotten it right on the first try.

It was the luckiest of choices for Benny. And it did succeed. The woman turned from the window and looked him in the eye, all at once and too directly. He seemed to her to be some kind of clairvoyant, like those big city fortune-tellers who stuck palmistry signs of the hand in their dead lawns—signs that said, "Madam Mysto Understands." After so many false starts, it rather scared Benjamin to have her full attention now.

41

"It's possible," she said.

"What's possible?" he asked, straining to tie their awkward conversation together.

"It's possible we've met before."

Benny could see her mind working. She was sorting through where they might have met before, or so he supposed. It made her uncomfortable to see that she was being studied.

His next guess was based upon a simple observation of her not wearing a wedding band. "Still single I see," he said.

She shuffled nervously.

The Bloomingdale's tag on her carpetbag that hung through the luggage rack caused him to guess, "And are you still living in downtown Manhattan?"

Now she wiggled nervously. It was obvious she suddenly revered him as a prophet. "Not anymore," she replied. "I moved." She was about to say where she had moved when she stiffened her posture and clammed up.

The single C of her monogram caused Benjamin to remark, "Still not using your first name, I see."

That did it. He was getting too close. She reddened as though she felt he really did know her and she wanted him to quit the examination. "Look, Mr. . . ."

"Baxter, ma'am, Baxter. I'm a salesman."

"Well, I'm not into sales."

Now she was talking! Benjamin Baxter knew he

had her. In fact, she wasn't only talking now but arguing. This was when he liked people best. Benny knew that when people got loud about their viewpoints, they were just about to change them. They didn't always know it, but they were, nonetheless. And Miss Cartwright was now engaged in an argument she couldn't win. She was about to buy whatever he was selling, only she didn't know it. Benjamin knew it. He had only a little more inductive work to do and then he could make the sale.

Benjamin Baxter shook his head slightly. Judging from her fishnet hose and overlarge rhinestone earbobs, Benny felt she was probably also a salesperson—but she was likely in a kind of sales that good city folks wouldn't much approve of. He had her on the defensive, and she was noticeably uncomfortable. He knew he mustn't ask her anything about her real line of work.

She retreated behind a defiant air. She must have decided she would lay down the questions and make him do the answering. But Benny could see what she was up to, and Benny knew that the best way to rebut a snoop was to snoop first.

"You sell Watkins products or Rosebud Salve?" she snipped.

"No, ma'am. I sell what all the world most needs and most runs from."

"Life insurance?"

"Well, in a way. I sell security, happiness, and peace of mind." Benny reached ceremoniously into his pocket and whisked out a business card. "Benjamin Baxter, ma'am. God is my King and Bibles are my thing! I'm committed to making the world better by selling it the Good Book! And while my name is Benjamin, my friends call me Benny. I'm in sales, and I make my living by understanding people. All life is sales. Everybody's selling something. A viewpoint, an attitude, a carpetbag full of pig iron!

"Look here!" He bent over and pulled out from under the seat a heavy leather briefcase. He unbuckled the straps and pulled a huge Bible out of the bag. "Here's what I sell, ma'am. The Good Book. It makes the bad good, the good better, and the goody-goody possible to live with. Like it says on the card, 'God is my King, Bibles are my thing!' " He paused a moment. She reached for his card. He grinned and held on to it. She tugged at it, causing him to grin wider and then release it rather abruptly.

She shrank back from the large book. It was as if he were thrusting a red hot poker at her. Benny had seen the syndrome many times before. It was the words *Holy Bible* that most menaced those who tried not to buy the book from him. And they were often more afraid of the word *Holy* than the word *Bible*. The word *Holy* terrifies the guilty, and Benny could see the fear in her eyes. She drew away, pushing herself as far back against the hard leather cushion of the train coach as she could get. She gestured for him to move back. But he advanced toward her menacingly, for now he could smell the aroma of a sale. He thrust the Bible toward her so that it nearly struck her. When he saw that she wasn't going to take it from him, he dropped it on her lap.

She looked down upon it with a kind of terror.

"Well, see there! It's lighter than your carpetbag, isn't it? My dear, you may not be aware of it, but you are holding a genuine *Three Generation Regal Heritage Bible*. Why there's enough power in that book to blow the corruption out of your life for the rest of your life. This baby's got thirty-six full-color illustrations, a bold-faced cross-referenced center strip, and a comprehensive concordance that will help you find those hard-to-locate Scriptures your grandma used to quote to you. And it's that new American Standard Bible, so modern you'll think you're reading Mark Twain and not Mark's gospel—I guarantee it."

It seemed pretty clear to Benjamin Baxter that she wasn't accustomed to looking for Scriptures. He continued. "There's a copy of this little winning wonder in the White House, and if Mr. Hoover had read it more, we'd all be depression-free right now. There are charts in there to tell you who the Hittites were and when Jesus is coming again, plus or minus an hour or two, mind you. Yes, ma'am, the *Three Generation Regal Heritage Bible* can change your future from uncertain to definite. Look here!" He pulled out a flier from the front of the book. "Here are the testimonies of movie stars, industrialists, and congressmen—both Democrats and Republicans—who have been changed by the *Three Generation Regal Heritage Bible*. Yes, fallen women and arrogant politicians have all been changed by this cowhide-covered book. So surely it could be of some use even to a fine upstanding schoolteacher like yourself."

Benny figured she'd never before been referred to as a "fine upstanding schoolteacher." Still, in his mind it wasn't wrong to be complimentary to the fallen if they ended up buying one of his Bibles. In Benny's mind, the end always justified the means. The key to good sales numbers was to figure out who people were and then upgrade their social status with compliments they didn't deserve but which might then pave the way to a purchase. He chased the little people toward a bigger life with flattery.

"Well, Mr. Baxter, I'm sure I could use it in my work with children, what with all the pictures it contains, but I'm a little low on cash, and my teacher's salary won't start again until September."

How quickly she had accepted his depiction of her. Benny could tell that she enjoyed the illusion of really being in the career he had given her.

"That's why the good folks at Regal have a time-payment plan, ma'am. You can own this $9.95 Bible for only $3.35 down, and $3.30 a month for the next two months."

"It would be good for the children . . . the ones in my classroom." She smiled as she pulled out a small coin purse. The purse contained nine or ten silver dollars and perhaps a couple more dollars in pennies, Indian-head nickels, and standing liberty quarters. Mr. Baxter received the money, jammed it into his pocket, and reached to take the Bible back.

Miss Cartwright looked puzzled. "But I just bought it!"

"Well, yes, you did. But, honey, you didn't buy this particular one," the salesman said. "Here, just fill out this sales contract and you will receive your own gift-boxed Bible at your home within two weeks. If you are able to pay off the contract early, you will also receive a genuine mustard-seed book-mark and a thirty-two page pamphlet on how to use the Word of God to guide you in your life career . . . of teaching."

"Yes, of course. I understand . . . teaching."

Miss Cartwright filled out the form with a pencil Benjamin Baxter had supplied her. Then she handed the form back to him, and he put both the Bible and the form back in his briefcase. He couldn't help but notice that the mailing address on the form was in care of Mabel Cartwright, King of Prussia, Pennsylvania.

Oh, that Cartwright, thought Benjamin Baxter. Christine was the name she hadn't divulged, and she was definitely no schoolteacher. Even so, he decided he must never let on. He smiled as the conductor came through the coach, shouting, "King of Prussia. Next station stop! King of Prussia. Next!"

Hard times shift the world into desperation, pulling the oddest families back together by common need. This is why, when the 11:30 A.M. train from New York pulled into the King of Prussia depot, Mabel Cartwright was there to meet it. Mabel had been losing touch with the world now and then—her mind refused to stay in the world at hand. Her mind preferred the world of *way back then* to the world of *now*. Still, it was the now-world to which her long estranged daughter was returning, and so she worked as hard as she could to focus on that world.

Her daughter had gone to New York in the early twenties and was now coming home. Mabel had received a letter from her saying that she would like to come home. She confessed in the letter that she'd turned "belly-up" in her finances and had nowhere else to go. Until her letter showed up, Mabel hadn't heard from her daughter in almost a decade, when she had left home to look for work in the Big Apple.

While Mabel had heard nothing from her, she had heard plenty *about* her. The word was out that Christine had never found "decent" work, even in the prosperous twenties. In time she had turned to prostitution to keep herself alive. Christine was her only child, and the news of her fall from respectability nearly broke Mabel's heart. For a good many years she never spoke of Christine.

Mabel's husband had died within a year or so after Christine left home. Mabel had been unable to locate Christine to tell her the news that her father had died. So when Mabel at last heard from her, only a few weeks earlier, her world had, in a sense, begun to turn again. Mabel was glad she was coming home. Whatever Christine may have been doing to keep herself alive, whatever condition she was in, the news of her homecoming seemed like Mabel's reprieve from an early meaningless death. She suddenly felt alive again. She had a daughter. No matter her past, she had a daughter.

Mabel had been pacing the platform long before the train arrived. Her mind flew through the vapors of happier times. She had been in her late teens when Christine was born. In fact, some had said that Christine was born too soon to allow the conception to be regarded as proper. But the early blitz of gossip had given way to a period of normalcy in both their lives. Then, shortly after the war, Christine had left home to make her way in the city and . . .

Mabel's eye interrupted her meandering mind. Soon her thoughts thinned away and were gone entirely. Mabel's mind more than meandered. Sometimes it just quit. She suffered a great deal from forgetfulness. This troubled her at first. Up till now she'd never struggled with forgetting things and so began to fear what could be happening to her. Her own mother had lost her mind completely by age sixty. Mabel still remembered Christine's childhood and all things long past, easier than she could remember where she'd last seen her reading spectacles. She once spent an entire morning looking for her lost dentures, grateful to find them at last in the cupboard on the back porch, though she had no idea how they got there.

The train was now on its way into the station. Mabel blinked, then smiled. She looked as though her sixty years were more like seventy-five. Her fine hair was gathered loosely in unruly wisps about her aging, thin face. Her print dress appeared as faded as her pale skin. Her eyes were dull and sad. Still, her whole sagging frame picked up a bit of starch at the arrival of the train.

Amid the hissing of air brakes and the gasping of steam, the train finally clanked to a stop. Christine Cartwright and Benjamin Baxter stepped off the train at the same time. Christine saw her mother and ran to her, and they embraced, although it seemed to Benny that Christine had more warmth in her greeting than did her mother.

Their first embrace was only of short endurance, until Mrs. Cartwright noticed Benny. "Benjamin Baxter! Good morning, and what brings you back to these parts?" Mabel's question was unnecessary. She could see his black briefcase and knew what it contained. "Still selling the *World-Hope Family Bible*?" Mabel felt good that she could remember both who Benjamin was and what he sold.

"No, Mrs. Cartwright, I've changed companies. I'm now selling the *Three Generation Regal Heritage Bible*. Once I saw this baby, I couldn't sell the *World-Hope* anymore. It just doesn't offer the help for the hard times that this newer Bible does."

"Well, I'm still reading my good old *World-Hope Bible*. It's in the King James, not that new worldly American Standard Version. Jesus just doesn't sound like Jesus in those newfangled Bibles! And I—"

"Mama, I just bought a Bible from Mr. Baxter."

"Oh. That's good, Christine!" She held her at arm's length and then drew her close and embraced her again. "Oh, Chris, Chris! I'm so glad you've come home at last." Christine could tell that Mabel meant it, even though the comment seemed more like a rebuke than a greeting. "We must go home now, child. Is this all your luggage?" she asked, pointing to the single carpetbag.

"It's all she has, Mrs. Cartwright," laughed Benny. "But don't belittle the cargo inside. You'd better hire yourself a strong porter to carry it home. It fell on me earlier and left me paralyzed for ten minutes."

Christine gave Benny a wan smile.

"Mr. Baxter, Mother and I have a lot to talk about, and if you don't mind, we—"

"Don't have to tell me more than once, Miss Christine. Hope your children at school enjoy that new Bible. Since that monkey trial down in Dayton, Tennessee, we need all the Bibles we can get into our schools. Moses and Darwin are in real disagreement, and these fancy-pants schoolteachers have nearly all taken Darwin's side. You just read and teach that *Three Generation Regal Heritage Bible* if you want to help Moses beat Darwin in the classroom."

"Thank you, I will." Christine motioned for a porter who brought his dolly and put it under the heavy carpetbag, then said, "Which way, ma'am?"

"This way," said Christine, and she turned on her heel to follow alongside Mabel as they started out, leaving Benny staring after them.

"Let's go home, Chris," her mother said.

They walked together, yet at a distance. The years of separate living had created a wall between them. Each had carried on her own individual life until the whole idea of togetherness became a notion sounding almost foreign. Their secret years had tangled like rotten cords in their hearts, which seemed impossible to unravel now. Each sensed it would be best to begin gently in getting reacquainted, to start by discussing the world she knew—the polite world, where people greeted each other and behaved openly. Mabel could tell from Christine's appearance that she'd made her living—or perhaps merely stayed alive—by doing what she had to do. And whatever it was that she had done, her Lutheran friends would never be able to talk about it kindly. Walking home, they talked on through the blistering patches of sunlight. They treasured the huge elms that dropped splotches of shade upon them. In the shade, the sun became bearable. In the shade, one could think about things cool and pleasant.

That night the estranged mother and daughter dined together. For Mabel it was a feast as sumptuous as that of a czar. But it was only the desperate times that made the feast seem so rich. Mabel had made them a pot of vegetable soup with a very small strip of beef and a disproportionate amount of potatoes. The depression had settled on King of Prussia in all its fury, and, as a result, beef scarcely showed up in the townspeople's stews.

The two women ate and talked. Sometimes there would be a lull in the conversation, and they would eat in silence. After a while, they would talk again as they periodically sipped their soup. Later, for dessert, they ate toast with last year's crab-apple jelly.

Each tried not to probe too roughly around the painful edges of their silent pasts. It was their first day together. Time was on their side. There would be little use in either of them making life hard on the other. They talked their way through washing dishes and spoons and pans. Soon the lights had to be turned on, then mother and daughter sat down together and continued to talk.

"There's something I want to show you," Mabel said to Christine and then rose and crossed the room to a large antique bureau.

Mabel produced an old dog-eared portfolio made of rusting tin and aging canvas and tied with a simple shoestring. The string was tight, and once released, the bulging contents of the portfolio sprang out as though they had been pent up under the pressure of years gone by. There were old tintype photos and small black-and-white ones that time had tinged into yellows and browns. Only her mother's interest in the photos caused Christine to in any way be intrigued by them. But then as Mabel proceeded to pick up each picture, turn it over in her hand, and pass it on to Christine, Mabel's repeating "this is so-and-so" and "remember when" took over the conversation.

Several times Mabel stopped her speaking rather abruptly and then looked caught up in her thoughts, yet her lips continued to move. One time she told Christine, "I just can't think who all these people are. It's my forgetfulness. Some days it's worse than others."

Mabel picked up a faded brown tintype and stared at it. Then seeing that Christine had observed her studying the old picture, Mabel hurriedly stuck the photo toward the bottom of the pile. Christine wondered if her mother hadn't just been caught in the act of some unmentionable memory—as if she were remembering something that shouldn't be remembered, or something she'd like to remember yet either couldn't or perhaps wouldn't remember.

"What was that one, Mom?" Christine asked.

"It was nothing, just someone I knew before I knew your father."

Christine wasn't satisfied, but she let the remark pass anyway. They looked at only a few more photos before Mabel confessed that she was tired. It wasn't long before both of them were in their beds, Mabel in the bed she'd slept in for years, and Christine in the bed she'd vacated a decade ago.

The day had been so stimulating that Christine found she couldn't sleep. As soon as she was sure Mabel was asleep, she tiptoed out of her bedroom and retrieved the tin and canvas portfolio and brought it back to her room. She quietly closed the door and switched on a small lamp, then began fingering through the portfolio, squinting in the stingy light to see the pictures. At last she came to the picture Mabel had reinserted lower in the stack. She could see that it was indeed a picture of her mother and a man who was not her father. The years caused her head to start pounding. Christine felt she knew the man but couldn't place the name, the circumstances. Then the fog drew back, and she remembered. The man in the photo was Harold McCaslin, the dairyman. She saw that there was a note scribbled on the back of the photo. "I will always love you" was all it said. The short sentence seemed at first completely unintelligible to Christine.

Toward the bottom of the stack of photos and notes lay a rubber-banded collection of receipts, written in varying amounts and signed by Harold McCaslin. Why had the old dairyman written her mother so many bank drafts? It appeared that for a period of months the man was paying her mother's living expenses. The dates on the receipts showed that the payments had occurred during the time just before Christine's birth. Also, there was a small piece of stationery that read: *Even though you are soon to marry Nick Cartwright, the child you will bear will always be a witness to our love. It matters not what the world may think, Mabel. I will know and God will know the child is ours. Yours forever, Harold.*

Christine removed the thirty-five-year-old paper and stuck it in her purse. She put the bundle back together, turned off the light, and opened the door. She could hear Mabel snoring slightly in the next room. Without making a sound, Christine tiptoed out the door and replaced the portfolio on the shelf exactly as her mother had left it. She then returned to her bedroom and quietly got back into bed. The bedsprings creaked, however, and caused Mabel to wake up.

"Are you all right, Christine?" she called.

"Fine, Mother! Everything's fine." Christine replied.

Nothing else was said, but Christine's mind

raced on. For years the rooms of that old house had been haunted by ghosts. She had accepted them even as a child, though now she had a piece of paper that explained some of the mysteries that had dogged her childhood. In the swirling mists of her memory, she recalled a tall man who used to come at odd hours—when her father wasn't there. Yet he always picked her up and patted her on the head as though he loved her. He always kissed her and set her down before he kissed her mother and left. Who was this mysterious man who stepped in and out of her home so suddenly and oftentimes in the dark? Why was he different from the one who was around in the hard reality of sunlight? Were they both real? Or was one the figment of a child's imagination?

Now she had the note. The mists were thinning vapors; the shrouded past had begun to emerge into the glaring, present day.

Benny the Bible Guy showed up at the McCaslin Dairy on the morning of June 7, 1930. He'd been there before and so needed no one to point him to the great white door of the old Victorian home. He straightened his tie as he peered into his own reflection in the polished brass plate of the door knocker. He spit on his thumb and index finger to coax an unruly lock of hair to lie down with the rest of his hair. Pleased with how he looked, he grinned and knocked with the brass knocker that gleamed in the center of the grand portal. It was Peter McCaslin himself who opened the door to greet the caller.

"Hello there!" the caller said.

"Benny the Bible Guy!" Peter was dumbfounded.

"At your beck and call. How ya fixed for Bibles, Mr. McCaslin? God's book of treasure for these hard times of locust and pestilence that the good Herbert Hoover has brought upon us all."

Benjamin Baxter believed that the evil days that

had recently come upon the world, along with their apocalyptic significance, could be directly traced to President Hoover. Benny didn't go so far as to believe Hoover was the antichrist, but to Benny's way of thinking, it was Hoover's baleful harlotries with the Up-and-Out that resulted in this depression.

"Well, Benny," Peter said, "we've still got the Bibles you sold us back in '26."

"You reading 'em regularly?"

"They're still in quite good shape if that's what you're getting at. So we have no need of more, I'm afraid."

"You know what they say—'A good Christian's Bible always shows a little wear and tear. If your Bible's in good shape, you're probably not!' "

"See you around, Benny!" Peter said as he rudely started closing the door in Benny's face.

"Hey! Wait a minute. Where's my little Dizzy Izzy?"

"Dead! Been resurrected as Isabel. She's done well without you, so go sell crazy somewhere else."

Benny shrugged. "She's out in the separating room, I'll bet." Benny could envision Isabel turning the crank that separated the milk from the cream. With that remark, Peter slammed the door.

Benny leaped from the porch and made his way toward the dairy barn. Still remembering where the separating room was located, he slipped quietly through the doorway and saw Isabel standing with her back to him, running the separator. He slowly stepped up behind her, reached both hands over her shoulders, and quickly covered her eyes. "Guess who?" he said, deepening his voice and imitating a Dixie drawl.

"Otto!" she said as she dropped the separator crank.

"Otto? Not on yo' laf, Miss Scarlett! It's yo true luv, who promised you he'd be coming back, who left this whole town standing on a stack o' Bibles."

"Benny?" Isabel said tentatively.

She wheeled around to face him. He threw his arms around her and kissed her brazenly on the mouth.

She tried to wrench free of his grasp, but he held on all the more tenaciously. Then she started beating on his chest, turning her head from his advances. "Help! Help!" she cried. "Let me go!"

Just as she cried for help, Ernest Pitovsky happened to be passing by the separating room and heard her screaming. He dashed into their presence and forcibly pried Benny loose and threw him to the ground.

Benny looked perplexed. He gazed up at Ernest and asked Isabel, "Is this Otto?"

Isabel's disorientation seemed to have temporarily subsided. Benny's letter still protruded from the pocket of her blouse. "No, this is my personal bodyguard, Mr. Pitovsky! And I'd advise you not to get fresh again!"

Benny picked himself up and dusted himself off.

"Well, Mr. Pitovsky, no offense. I'm Benjamin Baxter. I'm in love with Izzy McCaslin here, and when I get around this woman, I just can't behave right. You know what the Good Book says: 'Many waters cannot quench love, neither can the floods drown it.' That's Song of Solomon, chapter eight verse seven. It's in God's Good Book, and if God said it, I believe it, and that settles it!"

"Benny, you should know a lot of things have changed around here." Isabel said.

"So who you eatin' peaches on the porch swing with now, Izzy?"

"Ernest, would you mind helping Mr. Baxter find the door? He seems to have forgotten the way, and I'm busy separating right now." Isabel had steeled herself for this very moment, resolving that she would not let Benny get her mind out of whack again.

Ernest started toward Benny and grabbed him by the lapel.

"Whoa there, Goliath! Miss Izzy, tell this moose to put me down!" Ernest continued shoving the Bible salesman toward the door even as he pled for mercy.

"That's *Isabel*, Mr. Baxter. Go ahead and throw him out, Ernest."

"Whoa now! Please, show some hospitality, *Isabel*. Have you forgotten what the Good Book says? 'Be not forgetful to entertain strangers, for thereby some have entertained angels unaware.' That's

Hebrews thirteen two, Izzy . . . er, I mean, Isabel."

"Oh, all right. Let him go, Ernest." Ernest released him just short of having tossed him out of the separating room.

Izzy frowned. "Hospitality is here and now, but let me assure you, Mr. Baxter, you're definitely no angel!"

"Thanks, Ernest," Benny said as he readjusted his jacket and smoothed the lapels that had just been crinkled in Ernest's clenched fists. "Now, Izzy, where were we back in 1926? It's time we took up where we left off."

"Where we left off was where you took off, with your satchel full of money made from those family Bibles. You also absconded with all of my self-respect, which was pretty much tied to my confidence in you. I've spent four years getting over the craziness I caught from you. Go and make somebody else sick."

"I'm not selling that old *World-Hope Family Bible* anymore. I'm selling the all-new *Three Generation Regal Heritage Bible* with thirty-six full-color illustrations and a bold-faced cross-referenced center strip and also a comprehensive concordance. No more of that obscure King James muckety-muck. This baby's as readable as Mark Twain. There's a copy of it in Herbert Hoover's White House—and well-placed. This baby's changed fallen women and arrogant politicians into Salvation Army corporals. And it's

all yours for $3.35 down and two monthly install-
ments of $3.30 each."

"Good-bye, Benny!" Isabel turned and started
walking out of the separating room toward the
house.

"Hey! Who's been beatin' my time, anyway?
Who's this Otto?" asked Benny. He followed her out
of the barn.

"Otto Mueller," Isabel said, tossing the words
over her shoulder.

"The absentee son of the coal people?"

Rather than answering him this time, Isabel continued on and disappeared into the back of the
house.

Benjamin Baxter got a good grip on his satchel
and then walked right into the house after her.

"Now, you listen to me, Benny Baxter. I loved
you once, but that was over four years ago. I was
younger then, and frankly I could have been convinced to spend the rest of my life with you. But I
discovered that when a girl loves Benny Baxter, she
has to stand in line behind all the rest in every other
port of call. Let's face it, Mr. Baxter, any girl who
loves you would be wasting her love, because no one
could ever give you the kind of love you lavish on
yourself!"

"All right, I agree that *was* true. But it's not anymore," Benny said. "I've seen the light since then.
And once I saw it, guess who was at the center of
the glare?"

"Jesus, I suppose," Isabel replied.

"Well, yes, Jesus and you. I realized then how despicable I had been to the both of you. Jesus died for me on that old rugged cross, and you just lived—waiting for me in this old rugged gossip center of King of Prussia. Well, I got right with God at one of those Amy Semple McPherson meetings. I gave up selling that old *World-Hope Bible*. All I ever did was cheat the poor out of a living while I lined my own pockets. And, oh, I'm ashamed of this, but I did it all by pretense and religious chicanery."

Isabel felt he was genuinely ashamed. There was a tear on his cheek.

"So then I gave a thousand dollars to those poor little kids in the Philadelphia orphanage and another thousand to that wonderful woman of God, Amy Semple McPherson. I took the last five hundred and bought you this ring."

Benny whipped a jeweler's box out of his pocket and flipped the lid open. There glistening in the center of the box was the largest diamond Isabel had ever seen. The sun's rays coming through a nearby window hit the stone and sent a thousand glitters of light over the walls.

"Isabel, I have to have you. I have wronged you most miserably, but I still have to ask you—will you be my wife?"

Isabel was stunned! "I d-d-don't know!" she stammered. Her remote madness seemed to be returning now.

"Is it all too sudden for you?" Benny asked.

"Sudden? No, quite to the contrary . . ." She paused, then Benny leaned forward and kissed her again. This time she made no effort to resist him. In fact, she allowed him to do it. Then she pushed him back. "I need time. I must redeem the time, because the days are evil," she said, quoting from Paul's epistle to the Ephesians. While she had been responding in a normal manner, her eyes now began to take on that glazed look that made it clear she was shifting into her odd and broken state of mind. She was entering that hypnotic state only Benny could put her in.

"Well," he said, "you keep this while you think it over." Benny folded her fingers around the ring box and turned to leave.

"Benny, I'm sorry. Forgive me. I've missed you, like the deer that panteth after the water brooks." By now the old Isabel was back and fully mesmerized in Benny's presence. "I've come back to the well of Rachel and drink of its sweet water," she said absentmindedly.

Benny smiled. "Ah! That's good, my little chickie Bible baby, 'cause I'm also home where I belong. The prodigal is back. I've lived among swineherds, but I've come to the land of Haran to seek me a wife," he said, speaking the Scriptures back to her.

"I love you, Benny. I think."

"Think it not. Assert it. Be not double-minded,

for a double-minded woman is unstable in all her ways."

"Hast thou changed?" asked Isabel in Scripture talk.

"I've had my Gethsemane and met my ugly self on the Damascus road. I am a new creature, an ambassador of the Good Book. I love you as Boaz loved Ruth. Go not to glean in any other field."

"Look, ye maidens of Israel, it is my love. He is bounding like a stag across the fields." It was from the Song of Solomon, sort of. But Isabel's mind was too overwhelmed and confused to get it exactly right. Maybe it was from the scarlet woman who rode the beast. Maybe it was from that Philistine hussy, Delilah. Maybe from that awful Jezebel of Omri. Who could say? Certainly not Isabel. Benny was back, and there was a written rule that Benny and her better mind could not occupy the same place at the same time.

She watched him walk away.

Otto was now gone! His name didn't even come into her mind. Isabel hadn't thought of him, not once, while Benny was there. She hadn't the inclination. She looked down at the ring box and thought only of Benny. He'd come back to her with intention, and all she had in her once stable mind was now shrouded in a strange mist. Isabel knew she must try to think it all over clearly, yet thinking clearly was no longer possible. Benny was back!

One week passed before Hans left the Philadelphia hospital and arrived back in King of Prussia. It was late afternoon when his two strong sons steadied him against their own more willowy frames and helped him into the house. They hadn't been home long when Erick left to go see Mary, whom Hans no longer called the "Vithers vidow."

After he was gone, Hans spoke up. "I'm home again, Ingrid. Home is vhere, when you go there, they have to take you in." And then he added as a careless afterthought, "Home is vhere pigeons go to die!"

The last statement put Ingrid on edge. She couldn't deal with the idea that Hans didn't seem to mind the notion that he wouldn't live much longer. Ingrid could not stand it. "Stop saying things like that, Hans!"

"Like vhat?" he said as he raised himself on his left elbow, struggling to lift his weight from the couch's soft cushions. The maneuver wasn't achieved without a grimace of intense pain.

"Like that thing about pigeons," Ingrid replied.

"Pigeons die, Ingrid. People too. Ve all do, sooner or later—"

"Hans, I fixed you some soup, and you're going to eat it," Ingrid said, clipping off his cheerfully morose statement midsentence. She hated to see him looking so thin. His stocky physique had narrowed itself over the past few months. She couldn't bear thinking about where it would all end.

"Ingrid, I'm not hungry. I tell you and I tell you. Vhen vill you learn, I'm not hungry."

"You've got to eat, you hardheaded old German. Nobody can live without eating."

"Maybe later, Ingrid." But Ingrid knew there would be no later. He ate so little. His once robust appetite had been swallowed up by his sickness, and his not eating first manifested itself in his limpid jowls, which had thinned to a near hollow look. "Ingrid, I need another pain pill," he said. Ingrid could tell he was in great pain at the moment.

Marguerite LeBlanc, Otto's adopted child, had been playing quietly in the corner during the tense exchange between Ingrid and Hans. As Ingrid was returning from the kitchen with a glass of water and a pain pill, she was startled to hear Marguerite say, "Grandpa, why does Grandma call you a 'hardheaded old German'?"

"I think it's because she likes me so much, Marguerite." Hans stopped for a moment and thought of how puzzling this must sound to the little girl and so added, "You should hear vhat she called me back before she liked me so much."

"Here's your pill, you hardheaded old—" Ingrid stopped, glanced at Marguerite, and thought better of what she almost said. "I mean, here's your pill, my *darling, wonderful husband*. Wouldn't you like a little soup now, *dearest*?"

"Thanks for the pill, Ingrid, sveetheart, but I think I'll eat some soup tomorrow."

"Grandma, can I call Grandpa a hardheaded old German, 'cause I like him a whole lot too?" asked Marguerite.

"I think calling him 'Grandpa' will be fine, Marguerite," Ingrid said. "Now, let Grandpa tell you a story and then you'll have to get ready for bed."

"But I want to wait for Daddy to come home," she protested.

"It could be a vhile," said Hans.

"Yes, it's late night at the library, and he and Isabel are checking out some books." While Ingrid knew about Isabel and Otto no longer being a couple, she hadn't been able to tell Hans. He was just too sick to know everything. Ingrid couldn't bear to lay the extra weight of Otto's lost romance upon him.

"I vish the boy vould quit checking out books and do something manly for a change. Ingrid, don't you think they have an unwholesome relationship? Vhat red-blooded American coal deliveryman takes a voman to the library to check out books? Probably poetry too. All der boy does is read poetry and vork in the coal yard. Do you think dat's normal? Vhy don't he take her to der baseball game and den maybe out for chili and salt crackers. I vish he'd just let one manly belch fly out once in a vhile and quit being such a pansy."

"You old hardheaded—" Ingrid thought again of Marguerite.

"Grandma sure does love you, you old hard-headed German," offered Marguerite, patting Hans on his thin wrist.

"Marguerite, don't call your grandpa a hard-headed old German."

"But you said it was because you like him, and I like Grandpa too. So won't it be all right if I call him—"

"No, it won't. If you really like him, then call him 'Grandpa dearest.' Your papa will be home soon, and he'll probably bring you a book. But it will be late, so you'll have to read it in the morning. Let Grandpa tell you a story and then you need to get into your nightie and brush your teeth."

"But I want to wait up for Daddy!"

"Marguerite, you can't do that tonight. Do you understand Grandma?"

She did, but she showed little charity about it. Then she said, "Grandpa dearest ..."

Hans burst into laughter in spite of his pain, as

Ingrid turned on her heels and headed off to the kitchen.

"Just *Grandpa* vill be all right," he said, chuckling.

"Will you tell me about Hansel and Gretel and the witch back in Bavaria?"

"I vill indeed. Dey lived just down der street from us in der old country, you know." It was clearly an addition to the old tale. According to Hans's version, like Rapunzel, Hansel and Gretel had once been Hans's neighbors. Most truly noble people were once Bavarian children in Marguerite's mind. Ingrid knew he was embellishing things, but Marguerite didn't. And it did seem a gentle affliction to Ingrid that Hans pushed the story to insist that Hansel and Gretel's last name was in fact Mueller and that they were actually Otto's German cousins. But for Marguerite's sake, Ingrid made no effort to correct her husband from where she stood in the kitchen.

After finishing her kitchen work, Ingrid quietly invaded Otto's room to see if he'd left any laundry in his clothes hamper. Erick was better about taking his laundry to the utility room where she did the washing. Still, Otto's room was the room she found more interesting. The room felt like a monastery library. She never knew exactly what she would find, but half the time there was some freshly written verse lying on his small desk or nightstand. She was glad when Otto was out for the evening, for it gave her a chance to look about his room and see what might be lying around.

She wasn't disappointed. There lay a whole sheaf of pages and not the random selection she typically found. Instead, it was a manuscript, nearly finished it appeared. Its title was *Granite Daisies: Three Women in a Single Mirror*. Ingrid swept her hand over the cover page as if it were already embossed or engraved. But it was simple ink on simple paper.

She opened it and saw that the first section of the book was called "The Lover," the second, "The Village Oracle," and the third, "From the Beginning." Ingrid figured the first chapter would probably be about Renee, Marguerite's deceased mother. The second would doubtless be a tribute to Isabel McCaslin. She felt the urge to cry when she realized how Isabel had scuttled her dear Otto to the side and was back under Benny's dangerous control. The third section, though apparently unfinished, would be about herself.

Ingrid sat on Otto's bed and began reading at the third paper clip. She read, yet the words seemed to be too grand to be about her. She rejected the lofty sentiments that Otto had penned. Here and there a group of lines were so achingly beautiful, she retraced the phrases with her finger, reading them aloud and slowly, to savor with her ears what her eyes had refused to believe.

> "*Grace come womanward!*
> *Walk the heavy years and count them lightly as but*
>   *days,*
> *See not the Calvary of flowery fields*
> *You crossed on sunny Tuesdays,*
> *For some Madonnas die at once and have the*
>   *dying done with.*
> *Some die by decades and so redeem the years.*
> *As dying lovers siring crippled sons,*
> *They strut in thorny crowns with lives undone.*
> *And cruciform against the bleeding day,*
> *Build chains from tears to hold the night at bay.*"

Ingrid was so engrossed in reading she never heard the door close softly behind her, although she did hear the rumble of a man's voice.

"Oh, Otto!" she exclaimed as she spun around. "Forgive me for—"

"Snooping in my things," he said severely and then smiled. "To be honest, I left my manuscript there half hoping that you'd find it. Well, your critique?"

"It's . . . it's . . ." Ingrid was still stammering in the guilty embarrassment of having been caught reading in his room, "It's wonderful! But . . . Otto, this isn't me," she protested.

"No, it is not you. It is too small in its beauty, too stingy in its talent. You are so much more than this. But, Mother, if I could make my dull gifts find the words and increase the definition, then yes, yes, ever so much more than I could ever tell you, it *is* you."

Ingrid stood and Otto came to her. He held her for a moment and then he kissed her. "It's but the ramblings of a coal man, Mother. But its intent flies high above all it cries to say. Maybe it will have a worthier beauty when I'm through with it."

He hugged her once again.

"Otto, how are you holding up? Is Isabel still separated from her mind? Has Benny showed up at the dairy farm yet?"

"Yes, he has, and her condition is even worse since then. I'm afraid her mind will never return as long as he's around."

Neither of them said any more about Isabel's condition. After a long time, Otto turned his tormented mind to things more practical.

"Marguerite has fallen asleep on Dad's lap. I'd best bring her here and tuck her into bed. Did she want to hear Dad tell her of Rapunzel Mueller again, the prettiest woman in all of Bavaria?" he laughed.

"Not tonight, Otto. Tonight he told her of Hansel and Gretel Mueller, your distant Bavarian cousins," Ingrid said, grinning.

Otto laughed.

They both left Otto's room and returned to Hans's couch. Otto carefully lifted his sleeping child from Hans's chest and carried her back to their room.

Hans groaned in pain.

Ingrid decided to leave him on the couch.

She looked at him and noted once again that he'd lost a lot of weight. The hot soup she'd begged him to eat now sat cold on the end table, a wrinkled scum on top. "My darling, you cannot win this war unless you fight," she whispered. But she, too, was tired of fighting for that day and so she turned toward the bedroom. She would sleep alone tonight. She would soon sleep alone every night. A tear traced her cheek and fell onto her old dressing gown.

Otto's words didn't really fit her, being far too grand to describe her role in the Mueller household. Still, she thought of them anyway; they gave her a great deal of comfort in all she had to endure.

Thus cruciform against the bleeding day, she knew she must spend her tears to hold the night at bay.

8

Benjamin Baxter showed up at the Lutheran church the following Sunday morning. The sun was already unbearable at eleven o'clock when the service started. He hurried into the shadows of the great trees on the church's lawn. Benny could tell the sun was just too close to Pennsylvania. It seemed to burn the skin right through his clothes, making all decent earth turn to dust and the riverbeds into dried, cracked mosaics of mud tiles. But it wasn't the sun's inferno Benny focused on; it was the shade. He loved the shade, for it defied the sun's attempt to ruin summer. Shade was a hiding place, away from the scorching light that blasted gardens and made the paving a griddle.

Benny hurried into the church building. He knew that his sales in any community he visited were directly tied to his church attendance. Typically he started with the wealthiest and most prestigious denominations, except for the Episcopalians. Episcopalians—or "Whiskeypalians," as he often thought of them—were far too liberal to buy many Bibles. Besides, they were usually the best-educated people and tended to play down his sales pitches as soupy. Benny felt that Episcopalians sinned just as much as Lutherans, but they were always more polished about it.

No question about it, Lutherans bought more Bibles. Sure, some of them dismissed the importance of Benjamin's calling as a Bible salesman, yet many still had bought his *World-Hope Family Bible* four years ago, and he was sure they'd be interested in buying his most recent Bible as well. Benny paid close attention to all that was said in the churches he attended. In church he learned who was about to get married, who had lost a loved one to death, who had undergone a terrible season of financial loss, and who was suffering from illness or recovering from surgery.

He loved selling Bibles to Lutherans. They were practical people who bought Bibles because they liked the pictures, mostly reading them to gain insight, similar to the reason they read *The Old Farmer's Almanac*. Once he had called on all the Lutherans, he would move into the Baptist and Pentecostal churches. They also bought Bibles but usually on the time-payment plan, since they were unable to afford the whole of God's revelation at once. With Baptists and Pentecostals he always had to alter his sales pitch and focus more on the Second Coming and how close at hand it might be. He reminded them that if they hurried and bought his Bibles, they would probably be able to get both payments sent in before Jesus came again. He would then add that with Herbert Hoover in office and all the wickedness of those godless actors in the silent films, a person just never knew. "Besides," Benny would ask the Pentecostals, "do you want to be reading your old threadbare King James Bible when Jesus *does* come?" They never did, and usually the very picture of them reading cheap Bibles when Jesus returned to earth was an image enough to goad them into buying Benny's latest Bible. Benjamin knew how to deal with the Baptists, and he would do it later. But now he was checking out the Lutherans.

He jotted down a few notes while most of them were lustily singing "A Mighty Fortress Is Our God." *With these notes,* he thought, *I will scale that fortress and sell these people Bibles.* "Mr. Mueller is sick, not able to attend church," he wrote. "Mary Withers has a child that has severe asthma." Then Benny glanced behind him and recognized the man sitting in the back row. It was that Mr. Pitovsky, the same man who had nearly killed him earlier out at the McCaslin Dairy. But where was the man's wife? In a sanatorium ... *oh, very good!*

There were some obstacles to overcome with Mr. Pitovsky, but he felt the man was needy enough, which made him a good candidate to buy a new Bible. He found a prayer list lying on the floor.

Someone had dropped it—probably it slipped out from the pages of a Bible. There were six or seven entries on the list. His plan was to find out what kind of need was going on in each family and then call on them.

Reverend Stoltzfus gave an awfully long sermon it seemed to Benny. The reverend applied the widow's mite to the economics of the current depression and, by some convoluted means, ended up saying that the widow was likely a tither. Indeed it sounded like she was a Lutheran tither, faithfully giving her ten percent even in the hard times. So would any good Lutheran, the reverend said.

The sermon seemed to Benny to be pushing the Scripture further than it should. Still, Benny could understand about pushing the Scripture—he did a bit of that himself. Wisely, Reverend Stoltzfus applied the text to those who gave their money faithfully to God. Benny felt that when the preacher said, "You should give like the widow so the Lutheran church can continue to help people," that what he really meant was, "You should give so I can stay off welfare!"

That morning in church Benny spied Christine Cartwright and smiled at her. She winked at him. They had been meeting nearly every night at McPherson's Bar, though no one in the town suspected their affair. Certainly Isabel had no knowledge of their late-night relationship, and Benny was glad of that.

He also saw Isabel but avoided her eyes as she searched hard for a "hello." His thinking was that he must not allow people in the community to see him as being equally friendly with these two very different women.

After the sermon Benny greeted all those he knew and could remember from his last sales tour of the town. Most important, however, he now had a list of ten or twelve probable clients. He loved selling Bibles to widows, for they were always more spiritually needy than married women. After all, the married had their husbands and didn't need the Word of God as much as the poor widows.

There was just one final bit of sales research to be done. Benny stopped by the cemetery to read the newer headstones. His gravestone research brought him to the name of Tom Withers, 1899–1926. This would, of course, have to be Mary's late husband. It was a small, modest-looking stone. *A small stone— that's good,* he thought. *People who buy big stones don't usually buy big Bibles and vice versa.* And the man was only twenty-seven when he died, and therefore his widow would be young. He had also heard about Alexis and her asthma. With a sick child, the mother would be especially amenable toward buying one of his Bibles. When Benny's research was complete, he decided to start first with his last findings and so walked directly to the Witherses' house.

Benny knocked on the widow's door. He was surprised when it swung open and there stood a man.

"Can I help you?" said the man.

"Oh, I'm sorry," Benny said, "I'm looking for Mrs. Withers. I was under the impression that she lived here."

"I'm Mrs. Withers," Mary said, appearing suddenly at the side of the man.

"Oh, is this Mr. Withers then?" Benny asked, confident that it wasn't.

"No, but what a lovely dream you spin," the man laughed before adding, "I'm Erick Mueller," he said still laughing. Mary was laughing too, although not as vigorously.

"Well, I'm Benjamin—"

"Baxter," Erick interrupted.

"Have we met?"

"No, but my mother owns one of your *World-Hope* Bibles. She bought it from you some years ago. She saw you in church and pointed you out to me this very Sunday morning."

"Do I hear wedding bells about to ring?" asked Benny, changing the subject.

"We're getting married," sang out Alexis, who had suddenly appeared in the doorway with Mary and Erick, who both laughed at the statement.

"Oh, are *we* now?" Benny said. A stiff and awkward moment followed, and it became pretty clear to Benny that the Withers widow would likely not be buying a Bible today. Then there was little Alexis. "What's your name, sweetheart?" Benny asked.

"Alexis!" she chimed enthusiastically.

"Well, Alexis, what's this I see in your ear?"

"Nothing! There's nothing in my ear!"

"Oh no? Just look at this." Benny quickly reached for her ear. When he pulled his hand away, there was a quarter in his hand.

"Look, Mama, there was a quarter in my ear!"

Benny handed the quarter to her and asked, "Do you like Bible pictures, Alexis? I have a Bible right here in my bag that has thirty-six pictures of Jesus and other people of the Bible in it."

"Thirty-six pictures!" Alexis was nearly ecstatic.

"Would you like to see them?"

"Oh, Mama, could we?"

"Look, Mr. Benny—"

"Baxter, ma'am. God is my King, Bibles are my thing! Benjamin Baxter," he said and then repeated the motto on his business card even as he handed it to Mary Withers.

"We couldn't possibly afford to buy a Bible right now."

"Mrs. Withers, you can't afford to be without this Bible. It's the *Three Generation Regal Heritage Bible*. It's got a place to record your coming wedding and a registry for those who attend it. It's even got a page where you can record the date of death of your last husband and the wedding date of your next."

Suddenly Benny realized how crass that must

have sounded. He hurried on with his pitch to attempt to gloss over the whole *faux pas*. "It's got a registry of all your family birthdays and anniversaries—"

"Mr. Baxter, no!" said Erick, who then pushed Alexis and Mary behind him and closed the door.

Benny stood dumbfounded on the porch while still clutching the *Three Generation Regal Heritage Bible*. He was instantly angry and shouted, " 'Be not forgetful to entertain strangers: for thereby some have entertained angels unawares.' That's in Hebrews, Mrs. Withers." Then he muttered under his breath, "Snobbish religious people!"

He considered skipping over all the Lutherans on his list and going directly to the Baptists. But he thought better of it. After all, he still had the prayer list he'd picked up off the church floor. He wouldn't quit just because of one aggressive, negative man. He wondered about that Pitovsky man who had roughed him up at the McCaslin Dairy. He hadn't much cared for the brute. Still, he hadn't known at the time that the man had an afflicted wife at the Reser Sanatorium in Philly.

He smiled, stiffened his spine, and started off to make his next call. He had learned a bit more diplomacy since the last time he visited the dairy, when Ernest about threw him out of the barn. But then bygones should be bygones. Ernest Pitovsky had needs, and needy people bought Bibles. *Well, Benjamin Baxter,* he rebuked himself, *if you can't sell a Bible to a man with a sick wife, you're no salesman at all.*

Benjamin Baxter wasn't the only sales
agent in King of Prussia. Christine Cartwright was
bent on a sales program of her own. She felt her
mother had lived hand-to-mouth with little or no
respect far too long. In fact, her mother was often
seen as a nosy soul who by listening in on the party
line kept informed on the latest news in everyone's
life. She was a poor busybody, the least forgivable
sort of busybody. Peter McCaslin pegged Mabel
Cartwright, who now showed signs of losing her
mind, as one who was from the other side of the
tracks. This happened to be the Reading Railroad
tracks, which had set the social boundaries in King
of Prussia from the very earliest days the railroad
had come through this part of the country.

Peter had nothing much to do with anybody
who lived on the wrong side of the tracks. Mabel
Cartwright was especially beneath him. She was a
poor woman and had none of his fine breeding. She
was even further beneath him than the coal people,

the Muellers, whose relatives, Peter felt, had started
the Great War over in Germany. So in Peter's mind,
somehow the Muellers were indirectly responsible
for the conflict. Mabel Cartwright was English, and
while she could never be as noble as the Scottish, at
least she hadn't started any world wars.

That day when the brass door knocker sounded,
Peter had no idea how his world view was about to
change. He was astonished to find an over-rouged
"hussy" standing on the stoop of his grand home.

"Can I help you?" Peter McCaslin asked the
woman.

"Beyond all doubt you *can*," she said with some
finality. But then she added in a threatening tone,
"In fact, I suspect you *will* help me a great deal more
than you even now can imagine."

"I beg your pardon," said Peter, "but I'm not altogether sure that I like your tone of voice."

"I have not the slightest interest in whether or
not you like my tone of voice. My mother and I are
in desperate need of help, and I'd like you to invite
me inside to talk about how you can help us."

"What impertinence! Ma'am, I suggest you remove yourself from my property at once before I
call the constable! Vagrants from the rails are often
sobered up by a night or two in our fine city jail!"

"Call whom you will, my good fellow, but the
moment you do I shall certainly call the newspaper
and ask them to run these in the social register next

Sunday." Christine thrust a handful of old yellowed receipts at the dairyman.

Peter started to push her hand away when he suddenly thought better of it. He took the grubby notes and unwadded them.

"Notice the signature," Christine advised him.

Peter looked stunned. A long silence passed between them, then Peter crammed the unwelcome receipts into his pocket. "You will never get these back!" he yelled. "Now get out of here!"

"You do not think that I would be so foolish as to give you all of these I have. Keep what you will; I can assure you I have many more."

"What do you want, woman?"

"As I've already told you, my mother and I are in need. From all appearances you and your family are weathering these hard times very well. I want to talk to you about our survival."

"You cannot prove that these are my father's signatures."

"On the contrary, I think I can. The courthouse is full of your father's signatures that I think will compare very favorably with the signatures on those receipts. But if the world would not be convinced that they are authentic, I also have a photograph of your father and my mother together, with a very recriminating note on the back of it. The picture was taken before my mother married, but not before your father was. Now, why would your father have paid my mother so much money back in 1896? For the same reason that you will soon find yourself more kindly disposed to my mother and me. I would like to tell you all of this inside. May I come in?"

"Certainly not!" Peter was at the point of rage now.

"Very well," Christine said, remaining calm. "Then I'll tell you why right here. Had your father done the honorable thing toward my mother, my last name would have been *McCaslin*. Welcome me to the family, little brother."

The blood drained from Peter McCaslin's face and then his rage seemed to dissipate some. "So what exactly is it that you want?"

"Now that's more like it. The first thing I'd like is to come in, then we can talk peaceably about the other things I'd like."

Peter had no use for the disheveled woman standing on his doorstep, and blackmail was the last thing he wanted to be a party to. But to admit that his father had sinned or that he was in any way related to the Cartwrights seemed an evil smudge on his esteem within the community. He bore the weight of the heavy moment with pain. The world seemed to be falling down around his solid reputation.

"Won't you come in, Miss Cartwright," he said.

The devil had come for tea, and when he was finished, he would take the cup and saucer with him.

Isabel met Otto at the library. It had been their customary haunt during the previous months of their courtship. It wasn't just a cheap date for Otto, although Erick believed it to be just that. The library for Otto was a way to walk among great minds. It was a way to sit at a quiet desk with Thoreau or Emerson and have a wonderful conversation while the county tax board picked up the tab for the evening. Erick was the professor, but Otto had a natural love of learning, and Isabel, in the younger days of their romance, had been prone to love all that Otto loved and to express her love for his tastes as if he had commanded her to do so.

Still, while library dating had been their custom, this meeting was far from customary. So far the meeting had provided no answer to Otto's question of how to restore their lost relationship. Otto wasn't trying to get things back the way they were purely out of self-interest, either, though it was true he both resented and was secretly jealous of Benjamin

Baxter. But it was not his desire to compete with the Bible salesman. He felt compelled to try to rescue Isabel. He hated to see her so off balance. He more than anyone else in King of Prussia understood that Isabel's mental balance had been upset by Benny's return. With his arrival had returned the adjective *dizzy*, which the townspeople were once again applying to his beloved.

What was it that Benny carried with him that held the key to Isabel's fragile mental state? He'd met her when she was but an adolescent, still under the spell of her father's inordinate interest in the Shiloh community's preaching of the Second Coming. Her father's pressure, together with Benny's shysterism, had proven to be too much for her young mind. Most people thought Benjamin had taken over the work of making her crazy after her own father had died. But the legacy of them both was that Isabel read the Bible nonstop. Later she began making prophecies about when exactly the end of the war with Germany would come. She was so well versed in the Scriptures she could think up Bible responses to the simplest of statements. At the worst period of her lunacy, a common hello was apt to set her on a lengthy Biblical discourse.

But with Otto, all that had changed. Everyone in town could see it. Some even admired the "crippled Mueller boy" for effecting her healing. But Otto had never wanted to be seen as her rescuer. He admired Isabel for her kind spirit. Then, having been set free from using the Bible as her manual of fast answers to everything, Isabel seemed to have rediscovered the Bible as a kind of first-aid kit. With it she could bring a wave of genuine healing to the troubled souls she touched.

Isabel herself had noticed that the less she quoted the Good Book, the more it became a genuine part of her way of helping God's world along. What had most troubled Isabel was that some people who claimed to love the Bible retreated before its more difficult requirements. She couldn't understand how good church people could read it and then act as though its endorsements of love and service were of no real concern to them. She had experienced this especially during her attempt to help the Pitovskys. All of her fellow church members carried their Bibles to church but refused to give any help to this unfortunate family. Only the Muellers seemed to understand and appreciate her attempt to help the Pitovskys. Otto knew that her aiding the Pitovskys had been a merciful deed carried out by the one he loved, the one he saw as the new Isabel.

Now Benjamin was back. So was the old Isabel.

When Isabel had agreed to meet Otto at the library, he'd hoped this was a sign she was taking charge of her life again. He dared to believe she might be seeing the error of her ways now, or mostly the error of Benny's ways. But Benny had reawakened Isabel's girlish reminiscences and hopes, and once again her clouded mind lay as a gift for Benny's disposal.

Therefore, the meeting at the library only further wounded Otto. Isabel acted remote, clearly uninterested in restoring their relationship. An old man sat in the library within earshot of them, trying to read while Otto bargained for her soul. The man kept looking in their direction. Twice he cleared his throat, and the second time he also raised an eyebrow. Otto's fervent pleas were obviously disturbing his concentration. Otto took the hint. Rising from his chair, Otto led Isabel outside the library. He resigned himself to the fact that he'd been unable to bring her near, either to her senses or to himself.

At last he left her in exile under a streetlamp. He saw her standing there staring after him, her aloneness made luminous by the circle of light that held her form. As Otto walked away, he observed a series of lampposts keeping the darkness at bay. The streetlamps divided the world into circular bright islands of light in the midst of vast, dark oceans and the unseen. To Otto his retreat into these islands of light seemed a metaphor of Isabel's isolated heart.

Isabel stood there in the center of her small circle of light until Otto was no longer visible, and then she began her long walk back to the dairy truck. She'd left it parked near the old inn that had given King of Prussia both its name and identity. She paced through the circles of light between the lampposts and before long came to McPherson's Bar, the town's only downtown dive.

It is odd that a single glance can sometimes change one's world. And so it was to happen that all Otto had hoped was about to be borne in just such a glance. The windows of McPherson's were steamed up along the bottoms of the panes, but the dingy illumination of the place provided ample light for Isabel to see two very familiar figures seated on the barstools. There sat Benjamin Baxter before a half empty mug of beer. The beer was foamless; its white head had dissolved during the long hour it had rested before the slumping Bible salesman.

Isabel gasped.

On the next barstool was Christine Cartwright. Her mug was fuller, still crested with a thin line of white.

Isabel rubbed her eyes as if to make the dual demons disappear. But this was no specter. She continued to stare at them through the window until Christine interrupted her reverie by bending over to straighten the seams in her fishnet hose. Then she abandoned her barstool, stood, and tried to wriggle her overly tight skirt back down over her thighs.

Benjamin also dismounted from the stool. He patted her with a casual caress, which she didn't acknowledge probably because his caresses were so customary. Isabel would have been mesmerized by the entire scene had she not been so angered. It was apparent the two had come to the bar together and were now about to leave together too.

Isabel slunk back into the shrubs at the edge of the darkness as the pair stumbled out of McPherson's.

Then Isabel heard Benny say, "So she's your sister? Dizzy Izzy? And Peter's your brother?" They were obviously drunk. Benny had lost that crisp salesman's way of speaking that hammered out his pushy syllables with exactness.

"Yes, dear boy, it's true. We're relatives!"

Isabel tried to sort through the slurred words, to figure out who Christine was talking about. In but a moment it became obvious as she went on.

"Peter would rather it not be so, and he's willing to pay just to be sure the truth doesn't get out. Say, honey," Christine said, changing the subject, "it's too late to go all the way to your apartment. Why don't you just come on over to my house. 'Course, we'll have to be quiet so we don't wake up Mama. But the nice thing is that even if we woke her, she'd have no awareness of it in the morning."

"Well, my little chickie Bible baby," said Benny, "I'll at least see you to the porch." He stopped a moment and held her, then laughed out loud and said, "I still can't believe you're Dizzy Izzy's sister."

"You can't? Why, sure, I'm a regular blue blood in this town, honey. 'Course, I'll never tell a soul as long as that McCaslin money keeps comin' in. And you gotta promise not to tell anybody either. You promise?"

"Now, Chris, *your* little secret is *our* little secret. But sisters! You and Dizzzzy!" Benny elongated the word *Dizzy* with more *z*'s than Isabel could stand. "What a laugh!" he said.

"Is Izzy still crazy over the Bible?" Christine asked.

"Crazy as a loon! If I could have gotten her to marry me, I would've found a way into the McCaslin money myself, but it looks like you beat me to it, Chrissy honey. I gave her a cheap glass ring and asked her to marry me, but nothing I could say got me any closer to the McCaslin bucks. 'Course there's nothing like a little blackmail to succeed where a two-dollar diamond has failed."

"Benny, you're incorrigible!" Christine said.

"I don't know whether she got more excited about the ring or the fact that I told her I'd been born again at an Amy Semple McPherson meeting."

"And she believed you?"

"Apparently so. She doesn't sit with the Mueller cripple in church anymore."

It was the words *Mueller cripple* that converted Isabel from an undiscovered onlooker to a raging tiger. The fog of her dull mind burned away in the flame of her temper, and the craziness suddenly vanished.

Before Benny could grasp what was happening, Isabel flew out of the darkness and into the light. Although she was much slighter than Benny, the unexpected attack sent Benny careening into

Christine and then bouncing off a nearby lamppost. Both of them lay sprawled on the sidewalk. Because Benjamin couldn't quite regain himself from his drunken stupor, Isabel jumped on top of him and began pummeling him with her fists. She wasn't strong enough to injure him, but for a few moments he lay powerless to throw her off and stand to his feet.

Christine stood as fast as she could and strained to make sense of the dreamlike spectacle before her, that of some woman beating on the stupefied Bible salesman. She was too drunk to recognize Isabel. Terrified of Benny's wild-eyed assailant, Christine staggered off into the darkness and was soon out of sight. Neither Benny nor Isabel noticed Christine's hasty departure, because Benny was too busy trying to stay alive and Isabel too busy trying to kill him. Probably Christine had no desire to be implicated in the fracas, if the whole thing should be reported to the constable. Evading the law had been her life when she was a prostitute. She had learned to survive through escaping, and did so now.

But Benny wasn't lucky enough to escape. Isabel had taken him so off guard he didn't recognize her even as she clawed at his face and threw his head against the sidewalk. Then all of a sudden she was gone and Benny was alone, moaning on the sidewalk.

Isabel couldn't be sure what Benny's and Christine's odd conversation all meant, especially about

Christine's being a McCaslin. But whatever it meant, the only real barb in her heart was for Otto. He had cured her first illness. Now her second bout with *Benny-itis* was over thanks to this latest miracle of insight.

How foolish she felt. She climbed into the dairy truck and sat there, her face aflame, and shook. "Dear God . . . I'm so ashamed," she cried. She didn't tell God why she was ashamed, though she and God both knew it had to do with her stupidity. She had wronged a wonderful man, and she wondered if he would ever trust her fickle heart again. Now she needed Otto. Oh, how she needed him. Somehow she felt better. In spite of the pain of all she'd just endured, she knew she was better. She felt good just knowing why she felt so bad.

❧

There are some events that happen in the darkness, but when the morning comes the world is different, and all can see it. Even so, none but Isabel knew of the midnight miracle that had occurred.

Isabel woke up healed, yet she knew it would take some time for others to learn to see her as completely well again. Benny's picture was once again taken out of the pewter frame, only this time Isabel discarded it. She also removed Benny's glass ring from her hand and tossed it into the slough of the pigpen. *Like pearls before swine,* she thought. She watched the cheap ring drop into the gray mire and disappear forever.

It takes a lot of tears to wash away the lost dreams of adolescence. Who knew how much Isabel cried. She wasn't one to cry publicly, so her tears, like her healing, came at night. There was too much going on in King of Prussia to have anyone stop for long and notice Isabel's return from the tomb. But she was alive again, and sooner or later everyone would see she had risen.

When Erick walked up to Mary Withers's door on Saturday night, he was puzzled over seeing a car parked in her driveway. It was a very new Model A Ford, so late a model that its appearance in King of Prussia made the entire town seem old and out of touch with modern times. But these were not just modern times, they were desperate times. This depression, it seemed, was not going to slip away without a fight.

What a car! A real beaut! thought Erick. *It must have cost upwards of three hundred dollars. Who in King of Prussia could afford to buy a car for that kind of money?* The answer was simple—nobody. So what would this fine car be doing parked at Mary Withers's house? Did Mary have a rich friend she'd never told him about?

He knocked on the door even as he heard laughter coming from within. The laughter was cut short by the sound of his knock. Mary answered the door. "Erick, Erick," she said, saying his name twice as though needing to be sure he heard her. "Come in, come in!" Again she seemed to be speaking in doubled phrases. Had his arrival somehow addled her? "There's someone here you just have to meet. You just have to meet him!" Erick, overwhelmed by Mary's cheer, told himself that whoever had made Mary this happy he should now try to greet with the same sort of cheer.

Mary wheeled around, and Erick, still befuddled by her enthusiasm, followed her into the salon of her old Victorian home. As they entered the room, a tall man stood and advanced toward them.

Erick nearly fainted. It was Tom Withers! Square-jawed, rugged, and handsome, just as he had always been. And he was alive! How could this be? The whole town remembered how he had fallen through the ice and drowned nearly five years ago. Erick's face turned white, his jaw dropped, and his deportment fell to pieces as he struggled to make sense of what he saw.

Only it wasn't Tom.

"Erick, meet Ted Withers," said Mary brightly.

Erick reached and shook his hand. "Hello, Ted. *TED?*"

"Yes, *Ted*," Mary said, explaining what seemed a specter before Erick and bringing the world back into a rational mode. "It's so good to have him call on Alexis and me," she said to both men and yet also to neither of them. "I haven't seen Ted since Tom's funeral, and suddenly here he is back in the middle of our lives. Isn't it wonderful, Erick?"

Erick agreed that it was, but he was less jubilant about it than Mary was. "Am I interrupting something?" Erick asked.

Mary said that he couldn't possibly ever be an interruption, then added, "Ted drove over from Utica and brought us a box of sepia photographs of him and Tom. They were taken at the old place. Look at this, Erick! Isn't this remarkable?" It was a picture of two boys, identical twins—obviously Tom and Ted—sitting on a split rail fence.

"Remarkable!" agreed Erick, although he saw nothing very remarkable about the photo and absolutely nothing positive about Ted's visit that day. He quickly surveyed the other pictures lying about like playing cards between the two teacups that were also on the table.

In seeing him notice the cups, Mary suddenly felt embarrassed. "Tom . . . er, I mean, Erick, how about a cup of tea?"

"Mary, are you sure I'm not interrupting anything?" Erick asked again.

"Don't be silly! How could you ever interrupt, dearest," she said and then flew back to the kitchen to get all three of them some tea. Her absence made it possible for Erick and Ted to get a little more acquainted, but they seemed to be about as acquainted as they wanted to be. It was also possible at that time for each to notice that the other wasn't wearing a wedding band.

"What do you do for a living?" Erick asked. The question had come out sounding forward and impertinent.

"Whoa! You're an up-front kind of a guy. Never had much use for small talk, I see."

"Oh, I'm sorry. Am I being too pushy?"

"I work for myself," answered Ted, "still trying to make farming pay. All I'm really proving is that you can't sell corn to people who haven't got any money. But there's always plenty for us to eat."

"Us?"

"Mother Withers and I," he said. Then he sent the conversation flying in a new direction. "So you've been dating my widowed sister-in-law?"

Talk about cutting through the small talk, thought Erick, just before he said, "Dating is a pretty exalted word in King of Prussia. If dating means exciting theater or mountain-climbing adventures, the answer is no. But let me assure you, Ted, dating is too small a word for what I feel for Mary. I'm in love with your ex-sister-in-law."

"Ex? No ex. Once a sister-in-law, always a sister-in-law."

Erick had affirmed his love for Mary just as she reentered the room. He had spoken loudly enough for her to have heard in the next room or even the next county. Erick intended to be emphatic, to let Ted know that if he had any intention of moving in on Mary Withers, he could just forget it. Furthermore, he didn't believe that Ted had come all the way from Utica just to bring a cache of old family photographs. He could've sent them through the mail. No, this guy was smooth, a predator stalking his game in what Erick considered a no-hunting zone.

"And what do *you* do for a living?" Ted asked.

"I teach mathematics," Erick said, "over at Syracuse University."

"Do you always come to see Mary in the family coal truck?"

"Do you use that Model A outside to plow your farm?"

Mary cleared her throat. The uncivil probing stopped.

But almost as soon as it did, Erick cleared his throat nervously and stood up. "Mary, forgive me, but Papa isn't well. I need to be getting along." Mary rose to show him to the door, but Erick, walking fast, stayed ahead of her.

Then he quickly turned around and kissed Mary on the cheek. "Will Ted be staying long?" Once again Erick had spoken overly loud so that Ted might hear. He wanted there to be no mistake about how long Erick hoped he would be hanging around.

"I don't think so," Mary replied. "But he's asked Alexis and I to go back to Utica with him for a brief visit."

Suddenly Ted was at the door with them. He pretended that he hadn't noticed Erick's nervous display of affection. "I do want them to go back with me and see Mother Withers. It would mean so much to her."

You tinhorn cad! thought Erick. *You're as transparent as an unglazed window.* "I'm sure it would," said Erick aloud. "But, Mary, Papa's so sick. I need you right now. So does Mama. I hope you can stick around to see how things go. You've become the heartbeat of our family. I'm not sure we can get through this without you."

Mary smiled and said, "Now, now, Erick. I'm not all that important. Still, I wouldn't want to abandon Ingrid right now."

"It would only be for a little while," Ted offered. "Mary's had it so hard these last few years, she really needs to get away from this town and this old Victorian mausoleum of a house my brother left her. Erick, I know how much Mary loves your family, but that's all the more reason that all the Muellers need to set her free from any guilt of getting away from here for a spell. She particularly needs your blessing, Erick. Think a little bit about her welfare instead of your own."

"I'm sure Mary will do what she thinks is best." Erick said coldly.

"Erick, Ted, let me assure you both I *will* do what I believe is best. Somehow, Erick, I hope you will understand that Alexis really does need to visit her grandmother. I think that Tom would like that. I can sense him smiling down from heaven on the whole idea."

Erick gave her a second peck on the cheek. He felt the blood rush to his face as he turned and walked through the door and out into the cool summer evening. He wondered if Tom Withers really was smiling down from heaven on the idea. It was pretty clear his twin was smiling with his toothy grin from the doorway as Erick left. *Stop that smiling,* thought Erick. *And go back to Utica where you came from. We're all happy here!*

Walking to the coal truck, he could hear them laughing behind him, just as he'd heard them laughing when he first approached the house. Only now their laughter seemed wicked and inappropriate. Now their very togetherness seemed a curse on a young professor who had spent his entire life focusing on this one beautiful woman who seemed now to be pulling away. Was he taking all this too seriously? He remembered reading somewhere that only one out of eighty-eight births was twins. Even a statistic of genetics seemed set against him. He felt sick inside as he climbed into the truck. *One out of eighty-eight!* Slamming the door, he wondered again how the farmer could afford to drive such a beautiful car.

He backed out past the shiny car and felt ashamed of driving the Mueller coal truck. And besides all that, he was crying. He hadn't noticed it when he left the house, but he was crying. He felt as if he were at the edge of a dream, a *bête noire*. He knew why he was crying. It wasn't Ted Withers who had just invaded his life, it was Tom.

The one man Mary had first loved had returned in a Model A Ford, a resurrection of old dreams that split the tomb of her remorse. And Erick questioned whether this new enticement of all things old and familiar would be too much for Mary to lay aside. Her oddly disheveled world was being reassembled before Erick's eyes. "God, please help me! Send Ted home . . . alone." Erick's prayer was desperate, and just to be sure God was listening, he said, "God, listen up!" and then drove off down the road.

Isabel hurried toward the dairyman's shack. She had a letter for Ernest Pitovsky from Helena, his wife. Helena had made immense progress on her way to recovery, and there was little doubt in Isabel's mind that this letter, like the others that had preceded it, would be the best possible news. After her attack on the tipsy Bible salesman, she now relished the memory of Ernest rescuing her from Benny's forward advances. She didn't have to wait long before Ernest appeared at the door and immediately motioned her inside.

She was amazed that, even with Helena having been hospitalized for three months now, the tiny shack always appeared neat and clean. Ernest's face lit up when he saw Isabel. His cheerful reaction was always the same, though Isabel was the only caller he and the children ever had. Not only did she stay faithful in paying him for his work on the dairy farm, but she occasionally volunteered to watch Freiderich and Katrinka when he went to see "his woman," as he often put it.

"A letter, monsieur!" Isabel said, smiling.

Ernest grinned, then took the envelope from her. Isabel went and sat down on the only chair in the combination bedroom, living room, kitchen that comprised the Pitovsky family's living quarters.

Ernest eagerly tore open the letter and began reading it. "She's doing so well," he said after a moment. "The doctors believe she'll be able to come home as early as August. Isn't the Lord wonderful! And that's just about when the money will run out to pay for her care," he exulted.

"That is good news, Ernest. I'm so happy for you and Helena," Isabel said.

"Miss Isabel, you are the finest of people, except of course for my Helena. But I know that she probably wouldn't be alive today if it weren't for you." Ernest was a teddy bear. He couldn't compliment Isabel without his eyes filling with tears.

"Nonsense, my good man. God and you are the reason things are going so well. When she comes home, you'll be a family again. Won't that be a great day?"

"Sure will, Miss Isabel. A fine, fine day!"

"And just what is that?" Isabel asked, spying what looked to be a brand-new Bible lying on the small table.

"Well, Miss Isabel, that there is the new *Three Generation Regal Heritage Bible*. I bought it from that guy that was mauling you the other day in the separating room. It usually takes two or three weeks to get one mailed, but Mr. Baxter said that if I would pay for it all at once, then he'd let me have this one on the spot without having to wait. And besides that, because I bought it all at once, he also gave me one of those Miracle Mustard Seed bookmarkers. Helena and I have never really had a nice Bible. Now that we're all going to church it just seemed like that ought not to be so."

"But this salesman is the same man you roughed up in the separating room. What would possess you to buy a Bible from him?"

"Well, he said that the Good Lord forgave those who roughed Him up, and so he was forgiving me just like Jesus forgave them."

"But, Ernest, there are so many differences between Benny and Jesus, I'm surprised one or two of them didn't occur to you." Isabel stopped for a moment, picked up the Bible, then asked, "How much did he charge you?"

"He gave it to me for $9.95. I handed him a ten-dollar bill and told him to keep the change."

"Ernest, you are generous to the last. Who could fault you for that," Isabel said, determined not to hurt his feelings. "You've done the right thing and certainly for the right reason."

Later that morning Isabel began to feel sorry for all those the Bible salesman had taken in. She felt ashamed that she herself had been taken in twice by Benny. The first time had been four years earlier; the second had happened so recently she dared not think about it. So she could scarcely criticize Ernest for falling for Benny's high-pressure sales pitch. She had once felt the very same things about Benny that she could see Ernest felt now. Still, these were hard times, and while she wasn't against people buying Bibles, she was dead set against Benjamin Baxter's motives.

Isabel called Otto that afternoon, giving him the surprise of his life. She sounded normal again, and she could tell that Otto hoped she was. She was glad he agreed to visit her that very day. When he came over that evening, she could see he was surprised to see her sitting quietly and in charge of her world.

"Otto, about Benny—" She stopped midsentence in her confession of her stupidity. She was so embarrassed to have been deceived again by Benny that she decided to hold off repenting for now, setting aside the business of admitting her folly and explaining her recent trip away from her mind. She still was filled with a terrible need to get even with Benny for all that he'd put her through. So, to avoid the heavier issues, she blurted, "Otto, Benny just sold one of his expensive Bibles to Ernest Pitovsky, and Ernest really couldn't afford it."

Otto, sparing her the humiliation of all they had to talk about, joined her digression with one of his own. "He also sold one to the Jackson family, and they also couldn't afford it. Mrs. Jackson's children all had the whooping cough in May, and Robert Jackson hasn't had work in six months. But, Isabel, it's the most needy who are the most susceptible. Benny feeds on the poor and the needy. And let's face it, it's the needy who sometimes feel the Good Book is the only resource they have. They bite on Benny's corny sales pitch and they bite hard. Not only that, Reverend Stoltzfus told me that Benny offered him a dollar for every referral he would give him."

"The reverend would do that to his own congregation?"

"I don't think so, but Benny's probably making the same offer to every preacher in King of Prussia. These are hard times, and some of these preachers are bound to give in."

There was a slight lull in their conversation. Isabel's mind began cranking harder than it had in a long time. Then something subtle emerged. Otto knew her well enough to see some plan was taking shape in her head. She smiled and then closed her eyes for a moment. The oracle of King of Prussia retreated for a moment into that wonderfully complex mind of hers, and no doubt something was about to be borne. After some silence, Isabel smiled again and opened her eyes.

"Did you have a nice trip out of the present world?" he asked.

"The weather of the heart is always best," she said. "You're the poet—you should know that."

"Okay, Isabel, what gives?"

"Otto, how are things at home? How is your father doing?" she asked, once again completely changing the subject. Otto figured that wherever she'd gone in the silence, it was a kind of secret room, and what had taken place there wasn't something she now wanted to discuss. Case closed.

"Papa? Not so good. I don't think he can live much longer. He's in constant pain and hasn't eaten for a month now. I've never seen anyone deteriorate so fast," he said with a somber tone. Then he added wistfully, "But it's Mother who seems to have the real need. Papa takes the pain, manages to smile. In his own way, he's trying to get us ready for the inevitable. But Mama has been crying a lot. Worse than that, Isabel, she seems to be angry with God over this. In all the years I've known her, I've never seen her weep like this, and I've never seen this new hardness of face that seems to occupy her. I believe she is just plain disappointed with the Almighty. I understand her grief and her fear, but I wish I could give her back a little bit of her old cheer."

Isabel sat quietly for a long moment. "Otto," she said at last, "life is hard and swift, swifter than a weaver's shuttle, says Job. The worst sorts of things happen to the best sorts of people. The trials that come upon us either harden us or they soften us. When they make us brittle, we shatter. When they make us soft, we bend and maybe break a little, but the breaking is what puts the fiber in the tree and makes it stronger. They say that when the highland-ers need to find a walking stick, they go high into the mountains where the wind and storms have broken the thin trees so often that the heart of the wood is strong as steel. The highlander never trusts the flimsy, untried wood on the lower slopes. It's the wood that has fought the storms and lost that is the strongest."

Otto suddenly loved Isabel. No, it wasn't that he *suddenly* loved her; he had loved her all along. But he suddenly rediscovered his love for her. Yet he was afraid of the odd recurrence of her thinking tied to Benny. He now had to live with the fear that wherever she had just gone, she might go again in the future.

"I know what you're thinking," said Isabel. "You're thinking that I might lose my way out there and you'd not be able to find me ever again. Isn't that it? You're thinking that my recent departure might actually be a way of life for me. You're wondering if I might be an intermittent schizophrenic or something. I completely understand your fears, Otto. Believe me, I have faced this fear that is before you. I offer you no proof that I am completely well. Benny was the evil soul to which my father handed me when my youth was interrupted by his death. I believe Daddy meant well, but what he did helped to make me even more lopsided than he was. I wanted to please him, so I studied the Bible and took up most of his ideas, ideas that were only

reinforced by Mr. Baxter and his terrible salesman-
ship. Now I can see how foolish I really was. And
you're right if you think it could happen again. It
could be a problem for the rest of my life. It
could—"

"Isabel!" Otto said her name loudly, cutting short
her run-on confession. "Life comes with few guar-
antees. Who knows what any of us will be at sun-
rise? Madness is more common than plague. In fact,
it's a kind of plague. It is only the grace of God that
keeps any of us out of asylums. Each of us must live
our lives—all our lives—a step away from madness.
I'm sorry for your pain, but I'm not willing to let
what either of us have been, or for that matter what
we may be by morning, destroy our chances for happiness. Will you marry me?"

"Otto," she said, "I would marry you in a minute.
I've had no other dream than this throughout the
spring. But let us not hurry the date. Let us think
the matter through until both of us are sure that
we can live uninterrupted by the old ghosts that
have haunted our lives."

Otto could see there was wisdom in her words.
His had been the strangest of proposals, yet it
needed no other confirmation. Each knew it was
right.

They kissed, then Isabel said, "I must see your
mother. I must help her stand under the weight of
these days if I can." This would have ended their

conversation, except that Isabel felt compelled to say, "Otto, I do love you!"

"Our promises can wait, but even waiting promises should be three times kissed," he said. "This makes twice." He kissed her again. It was the kiss of a good man eager to keep his promise. "And now the third?"

"Oh no, the third must keep its distance," Isabel said. "Distance is no enemy to real love. It is a friend that writes the best definitions of love. So let us spend the promise as we wait, perhaps not long! Still, Otto, if not for you, for me. I need to pace our love. I love you too much to see you married to a person who can so easily lose her way and might make you unhappy."

"And I too have heavy thoughts to tend to. . . . Papa is dying, and Mama can't find her soul these days. Also, I can tell that you have hatched something in your mind that must be taken care of before our third kiss."

Otto drew her close and held her for a long time. It was a caress of confidence, affirmation, unattended by anxious or fearful thoughts. Otto's affection for Isabel proved to be a patient and kind and selfless love as only he could give, meant to serve Isabel and not him.

Isabel accepted his embrace, knowing his embrace was not an end but a promise.

The little world of King of Prussia was topsy-turvy with the sorts of little problems that upset such worlds. Isabel was bent on stopping a shyster, and Otto had the hard work of tending to a dying parent. Their final kiss could wait until their work was done, until their hurting, tiny worlds were properly bandaged. Then the sun of summer would hide its blistering head in the cooler shadows of the heart. They never stopped dreaming of soft, new September clouds and the coming of the gentle rains. In the meantime they must find some inner shade to hide them from any drought of heart.

Otto and Isabel were already seated

when Mabel and Christine Cartwright entered the church on Sunday. Otto was amazed at the transformation in both mother and daughter. For the past two weeks the name Cartwright had become a synonym for suave and chic—still a little lewd but far more stylish now. What Otto could not immediately know was that there had also been a sharp dip in Peter McCaslin's bank account.

And Isabel hadn't yet become aware that there was any correlation between the Cartwright's new deportment and the McCaslin finances. From time to time she was troubled by what Benny and Christine had spoken about outside McPherson's Bar on the night of her wild attack. What did Benny mean when he said, "You're Dizzy Izzy's sister?" Even so, she had no idea that Peter's stinginess had given way to blackmail and the extravagance that kept the Cartwrights from feeling the depression.

The entire church could see there had been a

radical change in Mabel Cartwright's appearance. The local butcher had noticed a change not in her appearance but in her buying habits when the forgetful Mabel had bought two pounds of pork chops and two t-bone steaks on the same day. Since the beginning of the depression, the town had turned largely vegetarian. And Mabel more than most had spent her pennies on soup bones and would never have permitted herself the luxury she was now suddenly indulging in.

Furthermore, when she went to buy the meat, she gave the butcher a ten-dollar bill and waited for the change. The butcher had never known her to have a ten-dollar bill in her life. The bill was a rare occurrence in King of Prussia. And the butcher could see a second ten protruding from the corner of Mabel's handkerchief where she'd been accustomed to tying in what little money she did have. After she'd left his shop, he watched her cross the street and enter the bakery and wondered by what act of God she was able to buy anything there.

But if her new flamboyance was obvious in the butcher shop on Friday, it was breathtaking come Sunday at church. Mabel wore a new beige hat with sequined netting, a stunning beige dress and gold belt—an outfit that clearly hadn't been purchased in King of Prussia. This could only lead her bewildered Lutheran friends to assume she'd taken the train into the city to buy the items. Since Mabel no longer possessed the mental capability to coordinate colors, someone else must have done her shopping. It could only be her newly returned daughter.

Christine was also more appropriately dressed than when she had first come back to King of Prussia. She still had a street-hard look about her, but her former uniform of fishnet hose and garish flapper sheath were no longer to be seen, at least on Sundays. She looked like one of the bad girls the Salvation Army had recently saved and then taught how to dress. Her dress was as appropriate as any Lutheran could ask. Yet her behavior revealed she hadn't been a Lutheran very long and that she had been accustomed to making her living in non-religious ways.

Reverend Stoltzfus greeted Christine and her mother as they entered the sanctuary. Peter McCaslin entered behind the two women and tried to pass the group silently in the aisle on his way to the McCaslin pew. Christine, in her own bawdy way, was proud to be a kind of flashy new Lutheran—a Christian with a diverse wardrobe.

She felt Lutheran enough to speak to Peter out in the open now, after their having dined with the devil in their more covert agreement. "Why, Peter McCaslin! How do you do?"

Peter nodded nervously as though merely speaking to her might in some way betray for all Lutherans everywhere in the world the ugly power she held over him. He moved on down the aisle. When he had reached his pew, he turned around to glance back at her, perhaps hoping she would just disappear. But she was still there and then horrors, she winked at him! None but Peter saw the wink, but he hated the gesture nonetheless. The wink seemed to say, "Don't get too hoity-toity, Mr. McCaslin, or indeed thou shalt be brought low."

Benjamin Baxter was right behind Peter, and as he came near Christine, she smiled invitingly at him. The smile was a bit too *come hither* even for Benny, who wanted her *come hithers* to be given a little more subtly.

"Oh, Reverend Stoltzfus, have you met Benjamin Baxter?" It was clear that he had. The reverend's wan smile didn't stop Christine from erupting, "He sold me this wonderful Bible a few weeks ago—the *Three Generation Regal Heritage Bible* with thirty-six colorful illustrations. I just love looking at the pictures. It would be just wonderful if everybody in our church had one, don't you agree?"

Reverend Stoltzfus nodded without actually agreeing to anything. There was something in the hesitant way he greeted Christine that said, "It would be better, sister, if you quit looking at the pictures in the Bible and actually began to read it."

Benny smiled, for it was clear that he agreed more with Christine. If Christine opened her Bible for any reason, even if just to look at the pictures, it seemed to him that was a kind of spiritual victory.

Christine sat through the church service but impatiently. She wasn't very good at church. She found the hymns unsingable. She filed her nails during the early part of the service, retouched her lipstick during the offertory, and looked at the pictures in her new Bible while Stoltzfus preached the sermon. But Christine's streetwise alter ego wasn't as apparent to her mother as to others, and so Mabel sat proudly beside her daughter throughout the service.

Otto and Isabel caused something of a stir by sitting together once again. They hadn't done so in recent weeks, not since their estrangement when Benny's old power over Isabel had exerted itself. During Isabel's wild excursion of mind, Otto had been sitting alone. Now it was Erick who sat alone.

Not present were Mary and Alexis. But Ingrid Mueller and all the rest of the "coal people's" entourage were seated in the back row along with Ernest Pitovsky and his two children. Ingrid, who could not fathom the lost intrigue and lover's quarrel that had separated Otto and Isabel, was glad to see them happily together again. What bothered Ingrid now was the situation with Erick. She knew that he suffered something more than just missing Mary and Alexis at the morning's service. She could see there was something of finality in Erick's dismal face.

Life had been hard for the Muellers, and Ingrid was in no mood to be sociable. She hadn't been to church in weeks. Hans was dying, and what she would have to face in the time just ahead had devastated her emotionally. She loved Mary Withers, but she now found herself angry over her abandonment of Erick. Why had she forsaken Erick at this critical time?

Yet even with her being in the most somber of moods, Ingrid had invited all in the Mueller pew to dinner after the service, the Pitovskys too. Although she'd become too dark within herself to be a very charming hostess, Ingrid welcomed the meal and the normalcy that came with it.

Isabel had prepared a casserole and a plate of salt ham to take over to the Muellers' for the dinner. Isabel could see how Ingrid suffered, how she carried a vacant moistness in her eyes that shouted despair to all who really knew her. She was a woman on the edge, and Isabel could think of nothing she could do to wrest her from the seizure of those demons she now fought with daily.

Hans was going to die. Ingrid could not accept this. Far less cheerfully than Hans, she waited and dreaded the days ahead.

Marguerite had to be told every five minutes not to bother Hans because he didn't feel good. Hans had been good about Marguerite's little annoyances, seeming even to enjoy her. Still, Hans was so tired, his once robust frame too frail now even to lift Marguerite and set her on his lap.

Hardly had they entered the house after church when Hans summoned up a cheer he didn't actually feel and called Marguerite over to the couch where he lay. He was so emaciated that even the patchwork comforter couldn't hide the sharp angles of his thinning frame that poked from under the heavy quilt.

"Grandpa, Grandma said I couldn't play with you," Marguerite said.

"And just vhy not?"

"Grandma said you are too sick to play with me."

"Do I look sick to you?"

"Nope!"

"Vell, dere you are! Nobody's sick unless they look sick." Hans raised himself up on an elbow. "Now, vhat shall ve talk about?"

"Tell me about the big snow in Bavaria," said Marguerite, repeating her knowledge of German geography just as Hans had told it to her.

"Vell, the big storm happened in 1888, or vas it 1889?"

"In 1888, Grandpa!"

Hans smiled proudly that she had remembered.

"That was in the last century, wasn't it, Grandpa? It was in the olden days, wasn't it?" Marguerite wanted Hans to know that she understood things like that. "How did you get to school back then, Grandpa?"

"I had to valk three miles."

Otto and Erick, who were listening from the kitchen where they were getting in the way of the women preparing dinner, both laughed. "Papa just keeps walking farther and farther through that snow the older he gets." It was an innocent statement, one they would all typically laugh at.

But this time Ingrid scolded them and said, "You boys quit laughing at your father." Then she turned away from them and began to cry.

Erick and Otto both felt terrible. An awkward silence ensued, and after this had gone on to an almost unbearable length, Otto approached Ingrid and put his arms around her. Ingrid continued to face away from the guests. "Mama, please forgive us, we meant no harm," he said.

Their attempt to get the world back within its orbit failed. Ingrid began sobbing uncontrollably and rushed off to her bedroom. Hans saw her as she passed through the living room and suddenly felt his own face flood with tears, an unusual event for the man who wasn't easily given to tears, even when his pain was unendurable. But the sight of Ingrid weeping was more than he could bear. Otto and Erick decided it best to let Ingrid have her tears and not attempt to cajole her into being the life of the party.

Ingrid had already set the table, so they all tried to get on with the dinner, but it was a cheerless affair.

Taking Marguerite and the Pitovskys with them in the dairy truck, Otto and Isabel headed out to the McCaslins'. Shortly afterward Erick went for a long walk, his steps weighted down by the afternoon's events.

Neither of the boys were gone long, and when

they returned home, they found Ingrid pleading with Hans to eat something. This time Hans gave it a try because he knew how much it would mean to Ingrid. Every mouthful of food seemed to nauseate him more than the last, and within a few minutes after he swallowed, he threw it all up again. There were more tears as Ingrid went about cleaning up the mess.

By midafternoon Hans was resting again, then Ingrid and Erick and Otto gathered together in their mother's bedroom to talk things through. Every word was purchased at great emotional expense, especially for Ingrid.

"Erick, we've lost Mary? I mean, you've lost Mary?" Ingrid's question brought only silence. Erick's eyes glistened. Ingrid then decided she mustn't pursue the issue any further.

After a moment, Erick pushed the conversation in a different direction. "Mama," he said, "Papa isn't doing well, is he?"

Ingrid shook her head and collapsed against his chest and wept quietly. A few moments later a deep, awkward silence entered the room, and it seemed they were all suddenly made mute, wishing to speak but finding themselves unable to utter a syllable.

Finally Otto broke the silence with words more unwelcome than the silence. He limped over to the two of them and widened the circle of his thin arms to include them both in an embrace. "Mama," he said, "we've got to prepare ourselves. Papa is dying."

Otto had supposed the words would send her into another volley of tears, but they didn't. Instead, Ingrid dabbed her eyes and pulled Otto's face toward her own and kissed him.

She turned away and was about to sit down on the bed when Erick said, "Hey! What about me?"

Ingrid actually laughed a little as she turned to kiss her professor son. "Don't give up on me, boys," she said. "I need you so badly right now. I can't find the old Hans, the man who was a stubborn, no-quitting old German. Worst of all, I can't find God. Every day in my prayers, I beg God to let Hans be just a little stronger than he was the day before and every day he is just a little weaker. I continue to watch him die even as I beg God to let him live. But God isn't helping me much. It seems Hans has just quit trying and God has just quit helping, and I can't go on anymore."

"Mama," said Otto, "there are times when we are powerless before the horrors of life. But you mustn't see yourself as the sole pilgrim through this ugly terrain. I watched my first love, Renee, die, and I begged God to allow her to live. I prayed over and over again the same prayer until my mind was numb. I railed at God. I told Him that only an ogre would strike Marguerite's mother like He was doing, that if he let Renee die and left little Marguerite without any earthly parent, I would denounce Him. I told Him I would rather be an atheist than believe in a God who stood back and watched beautiful young mothers die and their defenseless babies end up in orphanages. I went through exactly what you are going through. I begged and bargained with God to heal my love.

"Finally she died. And afterward I hated God! I held Marguerite for four days all through the funeral, which she had no ability to understand. Then I lost my income and had no means to care for Marguerite. When I came home in December, I was dangerously close to suicide. Do you know who it was that made me want to live again? It was you, Mama. You and Papa and Erick.

"You know who else I thought of . . . ? I thought of God. For the first time in my life I understood why God became a man, and then I could no longer blame Him. Heaven itself wept when His Son died, and God with all His almighty ways didn't prevent it from happening. God had to go through with it if He was ever going to hold out hope for any of us. My despair over Renee's death became an ugly bridge I had to cross into a tomorrow I didn't really want to enter. But, Mama, I crossed that bridge. Only then could I see God again. When I saw Him, I realized that He took no delight in my painful circumstances. I think that's where a lot of people get confused about God. They see Him as if He's grinning at our desperation. Not so! When I finally saw God, I could see that He was crying too. He cries when we do, Mama.

"He's like any worthy father, never hurting more

than when his own children hurt. But these lessons of the weeping God weren't available to me in the midst of my despair. They came only after I had arrived home and you and Papa embraced me. Only then did this confused prodigal get the proper view of all that God is. Once I saw the weeping God, I came at last to believe in Him again.

"We all sin when we act as though we're on life's pilgrimage alone. But life is a cradle-to-grave journey, and God understands that it's a journey traveled with many tears. Still, all must walk the path, and like it says in *Hamlet*, 'all that lives must die.' Papa, you, me, my darling Marguerite. Even my ugly brother here."

"Hey! Wait a minute. I don't mind having to die, but I don't much like being called ugly," said Erick.

Otto laughed, and Ingrid smiled at Erick's words. It was the first bit of levity in a while, and all three of them were rather grateful for it.

Then Otto said, "Know what I believe?" Both Ingrid and Erick shook their heads, indicating they had no idea what it was Otto believed but would both like to hear. "I believe that when you've lived a long time locked inside a dark mind, you cannot come out of it all at once."

At first what he shared didn't sound as deep or intriguing as Ingrid and Erick had expected, but after thinking about it awhile, Ingrid sensed there was something quite profound to what he'd said.

Nothing was spoken for a long moment, then

Erick turned toward Ingrid and said, "Mama, Otto is better with words than I am, and I won't try to match his reasoning, which was pretty good, big brother." Otto nodded his thanks. Erick went on, "But I had known Mary Withers for only a short time when I knew I wanted to marry her someday. Now I'm not sure if Mary is ever coming back to King of Prussia."

"Of course she's coming back. She loves you, Erick, I'm certain of it."

"No, Mama, you can't be certain. If you could have seen how Mary looked at Ted. She looked at him like he was Tom, like she was in love with him!" Erick grew quiet.

Otto and Ingrid looked at each other, not quite knowing what to say.

After a moment of quiet, Erick continued. "I don't know if we will ever marry, but do you know why I still think Mary is the most wonderful woman in the world?"

Ingrid thought she had an idea of what he was going to say, but quickly shrugged it off so she wouldn't interrupt his saying it.

"I know Mary has walked that same dark trail that you're on now, Mama. She lost her first husband and then struggled with God to keep Alexis alive. Some of her prayers God has answered and some He has not. Her husband is dead but not Alexis. And last Christmas Eve, which turned out so wonderful, I watched Mary deal with life methodically, practically. Part of the reason Alexis has survived is because when there was work to be done, Mary didn't rail at God but instead used what energy she had to please Him. Her work is her prayer."

"*Laborare est orare*," Otto said. "To work is to pray."

"Nice Latin," Erick said, smiling. "But honest Latin too. Papa *is* going to die. You don't like it or agree with it, Mama. Neither do we. Neither does God. But it's going to happen. Way back when you were married you promised 'for better, for worse, in sickness and in health . . . till death do us part.' So here and now you are testing the hard phrases of your wedding vows, thirty-five years down the road of life."

Ingrid had been silent for a long time. At last she said, "Oh, boys, God has given me so much. He gave me Hans. He gave me you. And so I'm going to help this dear man He has given me make it all the way to heaven, and with all the cheer I can muster."

They all hugged again. While they were clenched in a three-way embrace, Ingrid said, " 'I will lift up mine eyes unto the hills, from whence cometh my help.' "

" 'My help cometh from the Lord,' " Otto said.

"Amen and amen," agreed Erick.

They let go, and all three walked into the room where Hans was staring hard at them. "Vhat is dis? Having a little meeting to talk about how you are going to spend der insurance money?"

"Maybe we'll have a party and bake a cake for the undertaker," Ingrid said and then she laughed.

"Vell, Ingrid, if you have Reverend Stoltzfus read von of Otto's poems, make it a short von. Most of my coal customers don't understand poetry. Ve don't vant any of next vinter's purchases to be lost because of some long poem."

"To be honest, love, I wouldn't waste one of Otto's great poems on any of your pigheaded German cronies."

Wherever Ingrid had been, she was back now.

It was good to have her home again.

On Thursday, the first of August, two un-related events struck King of Prussia at the same time. The least significant of the two was that Christine Cartwright called on Peter McCaslin. He wasn't glad to see her, but he did ask her in. She requested a cup of tea, and so Kathleen went about serving her.

"I'll have strumpets with my tea," Christine added.

"I'm sure you mean *crumpets*, my dear," Kathleen said. But both Peter and Kathleen felt that Christine was more correct than she knew.

Kathleen set a small saucer of cookies by the tea-pot and left Christine and Peter to talk about what-ever it was they had to talk about. While Kathleen hadn't the slightest idea why this woman had now visited her husband twice, she held no positive feel-ings about the two calls.

"So this is how the rich live," Christine said, reaching down to straighten the seam in the back of her hose.

What do you want this time, you red-lipped hussy, thought Peter just before he asked, "Get on with it, woman! What do you want now?"

"My, my, Peter. Aren't we in a hurry? Do you treat all your family members this way? Just think, if our papa had married his first lover, I could have had all this." She reached across the table and tweaked Peter's cheek. "But *tsk tsk,*" she said with a sigh, "now I live across the tracks and you live here in this wonderful home. Do you think you could possibly invite me to your next bridge party so I could meet all your country club friends? It's high time I got to taste your caviar on my saltines."

"Get on with it—what do you want?" Peter repeated. He wasn't just being insistent, he was anxious to hurry their business to its conclusion, then hustle her out of his life as soon as he could.

"Just a little sisterly consideration is all I want. Would two hundred dollars be too much? Mama and I done spent what you gave us before."

Peter grimaced when he remembered he'd paid only a little more than two hundred for the family car. Peter stalked out of the room, and Christine ached to see where he went to get the cash. He soon returned with the two hundred dollars.

She thanked him and casually sipped her tea. "What delicious strumpets," she said, stuffing the money into the top of her dress. "Well, I can see that my stopping in for tea hasn't been nearly as pleasurable for you as it has been for me, so I'll just be saying toodle-oo. But only for a while, 'cause I know how much you love to see me come through that door." Then as she stood to leave, Isabel came into the room and was dumbfounded to find her there. "Oh, hello, Miss Izzy," Christine said. "I've just come to have tea with your brother, but the tea's gone and so am I, I'm afraid. By the way, would you like to have lunch with me sometime at Helga Bruenning's?"

But before Isabel could voice a reply, Christine was out the door.

"Why was *she* here, Peter?" Isabel asked.

"She wanted a job," he lied.

"She sure wore a lot of paint to apply for a job as a milkmaid. Don't hire her. Her makeup would frighten the cows." Isabel didn't care much for Christine either. Her reasons for disliking the woman were almost as intense as Peter's but for quite opposite reasons.

Peter could tell Isabel remained puzzled as to why Christine had come. He wondered if his sister might suspect that Christine had come not to apply for a job, but for an altogether different reason. Peter hated Christine more than he'd ever hated anyone. But he could conjure up no easy way to be rid of her. There were harder ways, and it was these that he focused on.

Mabel's mind was too far gone for her to act as her daughter's accomplice. So she probably knew nothing of her daughter's blackmail business. In fact, in just the past two months, it had become clear to most in King of Prussia that Mabel was rapidly losing all awareness. Peter wished she would lose both her mind and her daughter and be quick about it. For him it would be a double blessing.

After thinking about it awhile, Peter decided that his secret was still safe. He figured Isabel hadn't the slightest idea about what had prompted Christine's appearance. But Peter also realized Isabel understood how much he would spend to protect his reputation. He liked being well thought of. Sometimes it took money to be well thought of.

On Friday of the following week, Benny the Bible Guy went to call on the Magees, who had lost their means of income and had far too many children to take care of in the cruel circumstances of the depression. They were exactly the kind of needy people Benny took advantage of, and when he arrived to try and sell them the *Three Generation Regal Heritage Bible*, he was amazed to find they already had one. He asked them where they had gotten the Bible, and they told him that it was given to them by a very close friend whose name they were not at liberty to reveal.

Benny cursed his luck yet wasn't the kind of salesman to be easily discouraged. He called on the Fergusons next, who had been having family problems for years. To his surprise, they also showed him their recently acquired copy of the *Three Generation Bible*. Like the Magees, they too had been given the Bible by a close friend, and like the Magees, they also wouldn't tell him who that close friend was.

There were many within the Lutheran church membership whose need might have left them susceptible to Benny's high-pressure tactics, but in every case the new Bible had already been given to them. When he began working the Baptist and Pentecostal families of the town, he was shocked to discover that they too had been given new Bibles. Only a few of the homes he called on that entire weekend didn't already own the *Three Generation Bible*, and those particular families were not interested.

To add insult to injury, on Saturday he had received a letter from Ernest Pitovsky. Ernest's letter said that he wished to return his copy of the Bible and get back a full refund. It seemed that a dear friend had given him an additional copy of the Bible, so he didn't need the one he had purchased earlier from Benny. Ernest's letter didn't mention who had given him the Bible but just that he didn't need two Bibles so please send him his refund right away. Benny immediately sent him a response, reminding him in a letter that all sales were final and that his money could not be refunded.

It was soon clear to Benjamin Baxter that his Bible selling days were through in King of Prussia.

❧❧❧

At noon on that very day, Hans asked for two more pain pills.

Ingrid quickly complied. She could see that Hans was too weak now to hold the tumbler of water.

"Ingrid, I vant you to tell me again—" he stopped to catch his breath and get enough air to finish the statement—"of dat first day I saw you, at der park near der old inn."

"Hans, that was over thirty-five years ago!" she protested. Then she added, "To be sure, it was on a Sunday afternoon, my darling."

He looked at her and nodded, his eyes kind and alive with light. But they closed now and then as if the effort of holding them open required more energy than he possessed.

"You were wearing your lederhosen."

"Papa made me," he volunteered weakly. "I didn't vant to."

"Oh, but that's what attracted me to you. You were a pile of muscles in those suspenders and lederhosen. I remember I was with Irene Bagby, and I could tell she was green with envy when you brought me some lemonade. I was the envy of all the young Lutheran girls."

"You vere the only von dat mattered." Hans gasped as he struggled to gather more air into his lungs.

"I remember it was the last ice we had that summer, Hans darling, and the first lemons we were able to get. Do you remember how we used to eat the schnitzel over at old Bruenning's? He made his own mustard too, remember?"

"Bad stuff, too much horseradish," he said, somehow managing to get the whole comment out at once without having to stop for another breath.

"Indeed it was," laughed Ingrid. "You always said it was good for your sinuses. Then you walked me home late that night and I knew, Hans, I knew God had meant for us to meet and that we would always be together. And you were not only handsome, you had means. You owned your own horse and coal wagon. No doubt about it, you were the catch of the year. Later, when our boys came, I remember hoping they would look just like you. Nobody ever said they did. They said they looked like me, but I..."

She looked down.

She was stunned, for Hans wasn't there anymore. What she had so dreaded had come, and yet the dread was gone. He had just left her, quietly, in the middle of their conversation.

"Hans, I was talking to you!" she said, rebuking him for his all-too-sudden departure. Then she knelt down and patted his forehead and studied him for a long time. How she loved him. Love more than grief was her first companion after his passing. She kept staring at him for several moments and then finally whispered, "Go to sleep, my darling. I'll see you in the morning."

She folded his thin right hand across his thin chest.

"I love you, my darling, and I always will. Thank you for sharing my life, for staying with me all these years, for my view of all that will be, and for the hope we woke up to every day of our lives together. And thank you for the boys and for your stubborn insistence on doing the right as you saw it."

Ingrid folded his other hand across his chest. Then she leaned over and kissed him. "Good night, my life, my love. 'Many waters cannot quench love, neither can the floods drown it.' "

She stood and walked to the telephone and called Otto at the delivery office. "Papa's gone," she said.

Otto wept into the phone and said, "Not far, Mama, nor much ahead of us, I think."

Benny was feeling very depressed as he walked up onto the Cartwrights' stoop and knocked on the door. Christine answered the door.

Good grief, woman! Your lips are as red as Rahab's, he thought. But he said, "Good afternoon, Miss Christine. You look pretty enough to take to the dance over in Valley Forge tonight."

"Since when does a Bible salesman go dancin'?" she asked.

"I'm wrapping up my sales program here in K.P., sweetheart. Seems some other salesman has already been through here selling my same Bible. So there's nothin' much to do but go dancin' at the armory in Valley Forge before I move on to liberate all the needy folks over in Harrisburg. If you can't sell Bibles in Harrisburg, you can't sell Bibles, period! Those Amish lap up picture Bibles like a cat in a butter churn. Sure do hate to leave you though, sweetie."

"Well, if you're selling fun, I'm buying it. Mama

won't miss me. Let's dance all night and maybe even skip church tomorrow. Still, I've never dated a Bible salesman before. Can't imagine one who could dance very lively. Be like dancin' with a Baptist in leg braces." Christine laughed.

"Now, Miss Christine, don't you worry about that. I ain't always been a Bible salesman, you know. I used to sell bar supplies before all this talk of prohibition. Since the Prohibition, I've been stuck in *inhibition* and I'm ready to cut loose."

"Mind if I wear my fishnets and flapper duds?"

"Honey, you wear anything you like," he said, though inwardly, he thought, *That dress would make Jezebel look like a Sunday school teacher!* But it wasn't until he saw Christine in fishnets that he remembered what it was that both Rahab and Christine once did for a living.

For a Bible salesman, Benny got pretty loose that Saturday night. While he realized he was drinking more than "an Episcopalian at Mardi Gras," he remembered hearing somewhere in his stupor near midnight that there was a crazy woman over in King of Prussia who had been giving away free Bibles. Someone with bleary eyes told him it was that "Dizzy Izzy McCaslin." Yet it wasn't until Sunday around noon that Benny recalled with some clarity what he thought he'd heard the night before.

Suddenly he had a terrible urge to confront Izzy with the knowledge that he knew what she had done. After thinking on it, he decided to wait a bit, figuring it would be best to go and see her on his way out of town. First Benny wanted to make one final call on Christine Cartwright. He arrived at her house just after Christine and her mother had gotten home from church. He found them both crying, the house in disarray. The window in the back of the dining room was broken, and there was glass all over the floor. All the bureau drawers had been pulled out, their contents spilled onto the faded, worn carpet.

"I just can't believe anyone would do this to me and my mom," lamented Christine. "And they did it during church too. What kind of God would let this happen to me, when here I was in church being as faithful and pure as the Virgin Mary?"

It was an overstatement, but Benny let it pass. "I don't know, Christine," he said. *God's probably just getting even with you for last night,* he thought. He added out loud, "Now, Christine, baby, don't you cry. Sometimes the rain just falls on the just and the unjust." Although he wasn't exactly sure which category Christine was in.

"Is anything missing?" Benny asked. "They must've been looking for something."

"Yes, Mama's picture portfolio. It meant everything in the world to her. Now it's been stolen and we'll never see it again. Not only that but all of Mama's records and receipts were stolen too."

"Well, I suppose you can always live without pictures and receipts. Thank the Good Lord it wasn't something really valuable."

"But those pictures meant a lot, Benny."

While Benny had no idea how much they meant, Christine did. Her means of blackmailing Peter McCaslin was now gone and with it the power she had wielded over his life.

Benny felt sorry for Christine, though he could see his pity was unnecessary. Christine felt sorry enough for herself. What he couldn't know is that Christine Cartwright had just turned off Easy Street and back onto Depression Boulevard. Christine was weeping when Benny left the house. A Magdalene in fishnets, a Jezebel who wasn't weeping because she was penitent but because she'd just lost her way to make her wickedness profitable. Benny had left a lot of women weeping in his life, and Christine was one more.

❦

The Cartwright burglary was reported to the constable, but nothing ever came of it. No one noticed that Peter McCaslin had missed church that morning "due to a cold," as Kathleen told her fellow church members. When she returned home, Peter was feeling noticeably better. And no one saw the coincidence between Peter's having missed church and the break-in at the Cartwrights' house. Even Isabel seemed not to connect the two events.

Peter, however, had appeared strained when Isabel told him of the burglary. Isabel thought he also looked a little guilty. She wondered if Peter was somehow involved, but of course, she asked no questions, made no indictments. A while later she could tell Peter was happy again and had acquired a new vigor in his step. She also wondered why, after the Cartwright burglary, Christine stopped calling on the McCaslins.

While Isabel could never understand the power Christine had had over her brother, she was in some way glad that Peter was now back in the company of his own high regard.

17

On the night before the funeral, Erick and Otto and Isabel went with Ingrid to the funeral home to greet those who had come to pay their last respects to Hans. There were some who insisted that Hans looked quite natural the way the funeral director had laid him out. Ingrid took only brief looks and was convinced that he looked nothing like natural—nothing like the Hans she had known for most of her life. His bout with cancer had reduced him to skin and bones, and Ingrid now hated the fact that the disease had prevented her from keeping the robust remembrance of the man she had married.

Even though she would never forget the image of his youth, those days seemed so far away now. Had they once been young? Had she known Hans so long ago? Had she really loved him in her youth? Had he not been too independent, too brusque? Was the rambunctious spirit of his youth too far in the past to allow her to look through his opaque skin and see that long-ago leathery prince who had scaled the towers of her propriety to win her hand? No, this thin, dead thing was *not* hers. This was but the decorated vestige of her memories, a bad photograph of the real Hans. The figure in the coffin was little more than a poor, pale replica of her love—a cheap, pallid plaster done by a poor artist.

Otto too would not dwell upon the satin box that held his father. For his father wasn't a satin box sort of man. His father was a coal vendor. He had bent his back to heavy scoops and to the harnessing of his Percheron, Goliath, the horse that had been his workmate for years. Goliath was the kind of huge horse that Hans had to have. Any smaller horse would have looked obscene as it hauled the coal.

Ingrid was lost in a new aloneness. She suddenly felt a compulsion to act proper. But how was this to be done? How were new widows to behave, appear? Should they be demure? Were they permitted to laugh at a funny comment? Or should they not even smile? *Oh, Hans,* she thought to herself, *why, my darling, did you put me through this?* In the midst of her inner wrangling, she caught sight of Otto and Isabel sitting across the room. She tried to imagine how it was they felt. On another settee, between overlarge banks of funeral parlor ferns, sat Erick. How Ingrid wished Mary had at least come home for the funeral. Ingrid needed Mary too. How she wished she could have gone to Mary and cried, "Oh,

Mary, Mary. You've had years of being forced into the propriety of widowhood. Please tell me how to do it. Do I look like I'm taking it all too easily? Should I appear more grim? Help me."

At length Ingrid made her way to Erick. "Erick," she said, "it's going to be up to you and Otto to help me to learn how to be alone, how to appear strong and not look so confused."

"Mama, you are to me so much more than you can ever know. Life has a way of making us forget how we felt about coping with death. Please, only celebrate Papa right now. Don't worry about how you appear. You could be nothing less than beautiful and proper to anyone who really knows you."

Ingrid felt overwhelmed with both gratitude and grief as she held on to Erick for a very long time and sobbed. After she finally loosened her hold, she kissed him on the neck and asked, "Erick, when you first saw your father in the coffin, did you have the odd sensation that it wasn't really him?"

"Of course, Mama," he answered. "Could a Christian ever feel any other way? And yet you know, Mama, I somehow wanted to crawl in the box and be buried with him. I wish Mary were here."

Mary wasn't.

The moment of Erick's wishing soon became lost as he greeted other guests who had arrived at the last possible moment. In spite of Erick's counsel, Ingrid felt that familiar uneasiness of soul each time she greeted one of Hans's friends. By 8:30 P.M. all had left, and Ingrid was thankful she and her sons could now leave the mortuary. They talked quietly all the way home, speaking mostly of the funeral service to come.

Family. This was the greatest of all God's gifts. And strong sons to lean on. For Ingrid, a brilliant son with a brilliant mind who would help her figure out how to live without Hans. Also, a son who was a singer, who would give her a song to help her through the shadowy trials that would flank the narrow valleys she would have to negotiate. She loved them, not just because they were her boys, but because each in his own way had proved himself a pillar of truth and loyalty. *Hans,* she thought, *I will miss you, but I will make it.*

Soon they were standing in front of the house. They slowly stepped inside. There were no coats to hang; the terribly hot weather forbade it. Being tired of coffee and assuming Erick and Otto were also, Ingrid went ahead and sliced a lemon and made some iced tea. It was the simplest of fare. No one was hungry, least of all her. They drank their tea in silence.

Ingrid then went to her bedroom, got out of her black dress, and slipped into a sheer gown. The thin material felt cool and refreshing on her skin. It was too warm to wear anything else. She turned out the light and got into bed. Suddenly she remembered she was alone. The tears came once again. She didn't try to stop them. Rather, she tried to pray, yet God seemed to be busy with other human tragedies at the moment. Feeling desperate, she called out through the darkness to her lifelong friend. "Hans, am I doing wrong or right? I hate making these decisions all by myself." She thought for a second that Hans wasn't open to talking to her anymore, but then she was startled to hear him. He seemed to say, *Ingrid, you always vere a little pushy. You need to make a little space for der boys to take a swing at life on their own. Everything vill vork out, Ingrid, but you can't hurry dese things, you know.*

Ingrid quit crying and then struggled to imagine the empty bed filled again with Hans's huge hulk and her needy soul finding itself all wrapped up in his arms. But it was no use—the bed was empty. "Hans, how can I stand this?" she asked. But Hans was silent. He'd always been a man of few words, and he didn't say anything else that evening. Ingrid spent many tears as she tried to push back the lonely night. Grief gave way to numbness as she waited for the tardy sun to rise.

Hans was more beloved than he could ever have imagined. Ingrid had asked Reverend Stoltzfus if Otto could do the eulogy. The church was banked with flowers, and the pews were packed with mourners. The pallbearers were all long-standing members of the church, and as usual, Gilda Ammerding sat at the organ. The music was a collage of old German hymns, and as hymns went, they were among Hans's favorites. Hans, however, did not generally like hymns. He always felt they were in the way of getting down to the sermon, which, he used to say, was "vhy people go to church in der first place."

Not only were hymns not to Hans's liking, neither was poetry. And hymns, according to Hans, were only poems that people sang. But hymns and poetry are the stuff of all funerals, and so they were of Hans's. Reverend Stoltzfus read the obituary and moderated the flow of the service, but other than that he had no major part in the service.

Erick read the Scriptures. " 'The Lord is my shepherd . . .' " " 'Naked came I out of my mother's womb, and naked shall I return thither: the Lord gave, and the Lord hath taken away; blessed be the name of the Lord.' " " 'So teach us to number our days, that we may apply our hearts unto wisdom.' " He also read, " 'In my Father's house are many mansions. . . .' " " 'I am now ready to be offered, and the time of my departure is at hand. I have fought a good fight, I have finished my course, I have kept the faith: Henceforth there is laid up for me a crown of righteousness, which the Lord, the righteous judge, shall give me at that day: and not to me only, but unto all them also that love his appearing.' "

But Otto's words were those that kept Ingrid's heart from slipping into the numbness that threatened as she was forced to live through the funeral. Otto told of his love for his father, of the quarrel that had once separated them, and of his wonderful homecoming later. He spoke of Hans's embrace, the warm hug of a big man whose chest and arms could collect and absorb all the fears that had threatened his children. He spoke of the security of a man who understood that he was responsible for his family and who took those responsibilities seriously. He told of a man who wrapped his self-doubt in his next day's work, who kept his tears on the inside, because tears and fears can be contagious and he didn't want his family to feel the anxiety he had lived with during hard times. He spoke of a man who wasn't ashamed to love a grandchild that came to him from beyond his German heritage, a heritage many immigrants have cherished to a fault.

He described the humor that was always one of the ingredients of their days together.

Then Otto gave his gift of words to all who would consider them a gift.

"Dying is the end of nothing in the overcoming life;
Still it is living's only emptiness until life
     overcomes its fear of death.
It is death which teaches us that immortality is but
     the final expression of God's nearness.
Papa's family was his calling.
Warming the world, his ministry.
He bent his back to scooping coal
And drove the cold of life away.
Yet never did he see his miracle of warmth.
Flimsy sentiment found no thread in the twill of
     his coarse cloth.
There were words he couldn't say aloud:
Love, grace, inwardness, duty, help me.
He feared such words
Lest their undressed protocol should steal his
     manliness.
He was not one to make a public show of prayer.
Still he made sure prayers were said ahead of every
     meal.
He walked with God, but they neither of them
     chattered as they
Strolled the years.
Yet he and God were quiet friends."

"Good-bye, Papa. Winter has come early. Make heaven warm till we arrive."

Otto's eulogy was finished, his face wet. He walked over and sat down by Ingrid. Her face, like his, glistened beneath her black-netted veil. The emotion turned the scene to temporary stone. All was silent.

After a while, the mortician cleared his throat nervously, and the world stunned silent by love came suddenly alive again. The pallbearers stood to their feet, and then Reverend Stoltzfus quickly sprang up too. The reverend appeared awkward, it probably dawning on him that he was in charge here and there were things to do. Therefore, he led the queue of pallbearers down the center aisle, with the ushers following behind after all of them had passed.

Hans was buried in the churchyard. The thin, black serpentine line of mourners threaded through the gravestones and formed a sullen circle around the six-foot-deep hole where Hans would be laid to rest, to "await the trumpet," as Reverend Stoltzfus put it.

More Scriptures were read and then the committal prayer.

Reverend Stoltzfus finished by quoting Alfred Tennyson:

"Twilight and evening bell,
And after that the dark!

And may there be no sadness of farewell,
When I embark."

The reverend then picked a rose from a spray of flowers and handed it to Ingrid. It was a flower already cut from its stem of life. It too was dying, and Ingrid could see that the entire world was at some stage of dying. The trick was to make it live as long as possible and then give it up in hope, believing that real life was born long ago in an empty Judean tomb. Hans had more of that life than most knew.

When Ingrid turned to leave the canopy of the funeral tent, her eye caught sight of Mary Withers. Ingrid gave her a smile. They were too far apart from each other to speak. Besides, Mary was arm in arm with Ted Withers, her brother-in-law. Erick, who had taken Ingrid's arm, had also seen Mary and Ted. Erick felt a most unmanly stinging in his eyes. Ingrid wished that Mary could have been with them, but she was not. Mary seemed to carry too much guilt about being with Ted to speak to the family. She probably realized that her being with Ted was too much of a burden to allow the Muellers any comfort right now, and yet to bring comfort was the very reason she had most likely come.

Erick saw them getting into Ted's Ford. Then they were gone. Erick's grief was made double as he watched them drive away. His heart would retain the fractures of that summer, and he felt his hurt would never heal.

Following the service was a dinner at the church. Friends of years gone by fluttered around Ingrid, saying "I'm sorry" and "If there's anything I can do" and "He looked so natural lying there" and "It was a meaningful service." This was the accompaniment to bowls of potato salad and a salty ham—something quite uncommon during this depression.

Ingrid and her sons and Marguerite walked home together. Marguerite wore an older pinafore, but in her own mind she was smartly dressed. Once home their conversation turned again to life as it now was.

It was hot, the sun was shining bright. Ingrid glanced out the window, and her eyes fell on the old sundial. But the sun created the shade of hope, a cooler place where life could look to the future perhaps. The arrogant stylus stood straight up, casting its knife-edged shadow on the Roman numeral six. *Life has hurried us all ahead today,* she said to herself.

Then her eyes beheld the inscription around the face of the green bronze dial. "Lord, teach us to number our days." Ingrid felt a bright seizure of emotion in the center of her soul. *Hans, my darling, your numbering is over now.*

By evening Ingrid had put aside her reveries and was busy helping Marguerite dress for bed. After they had said their prayers together and Ingrid tucked Marguerite into her bed, Marguerite looked up at her grandma and asked, "Grandpa's in heaven now, isn't he?"

"Yes, Marguerite," replied Ingrid.

"And now Papa and Uncle Erick and I will have to stay very close to you."

"Yes, Marguerite. You will have to stay very close indeed."

"That's what Papa said too."

"Your papa is right. With Grandpa in heaven now, you're all I have left, and I'll need you to love me very hard, or I won't be able to make it."

"Is heaven pretty, Grandma?"

"Very, very pretty."

"And Jesus is there?"

"He is, Marguerite."

With that, the conversation ended, and soon Marguerite was asleep. The house seemed unusually quiet. The cooling shadows of the night caused the old house to creak. "Hans," she whispered, "I have lived for you for thirty-five years. What am I to live for now?"

Vell, Ingrid, vhat am I supposed to do? I can't leave heaven, and things are better here than I thought dey vould be. Do der best you can. I'll be here vaiting and I'll never quit loving you.

Ingrid ceased talking.

So did Hans.

Otto called on Isabel with intention. A week had passed since Hans's funeral, and Otto felt that it was time he popped the question and certified Isabel's answer with the proper jewelry. He had the ring in his pocket. Isabel had finished supervising the day's milking, and Otto was all through with the coal business for the day. There was still adequate time for iced tea. The apples were ready for pie now, and she'd just taken a beautiful apple cobbler from the oven. Always available at the McCaslin Dairy was cold, rich cream, and the cobbler came drenched in this richness.

The porch swing was the perfect place to share the freshly made treat. When they pushed back on the swing and lifted their feet, they felt themselves aloft, moving through an exotic summer breeze that moved them forward together. Love and apple cobbler could lift them into the gentle air of the evening shade. They each exulted in the other's nearness.

While the swing moved rhythmically ahead and back, Otto's attention turned to Benny the Bible Guy. He wanted to be sure there were no skeletons lingering in Isabel's romantic closet.

He knew that Isabel's crusades were sometimes quiet yet they were always intense. He listened as she explained how she had outwitted Benny. From the copyright page of Ernest Pitovsky's new Bible she'd discovered that the Bibles Benny was selling were printed in Philadelphia. Once she knew that, she drove the dairy truck to the publisher and signed on as a salesperson.

"You know," Isabel said, "Benny was buying those Bibles for only a dollar-fifty and selling them for ten! Worst of all, he was picking on those who could least afford his extravagant price. I had only to think through who Benny's customers might be and then get there ahead of him to sell the Bibles at cost. If people couldn't afford them at all, I simply gave them a Bible."

Otto nodded. "People say they left town to-gether—Benny and Christine." But then Otto stopped this line of thought and started another. "What do you make of the break-in at Mabel Cartwright's house during church services?"

"It was highly irregular. No money was taken and nothing stolen but a picture portfolio. Who would want a bunch of pictures of Mabel Cartwright?"

"This is the most disjointed summer I can remember," Otto said. "Although I've been out of town for a decade or more."

The statement stood alone and was followed by nothing but quietness for a moment before Isabel changed the subject by erupting, "Helena Pitovsky is coming home next week!"

"Wonderful! Oh, how much the Pitovskys owe you, Isabel."

"Nonsense! We're all the children of God. I was only giving the Good Lord a chance to work a simple miracle. I've found it doesn't take much of a miracle to astound Lutherans." Isabel was acting a bit self-excusing and Otto knew it.

"It's amazing how miracles are best born when there's someone around who is open to kindness," Otto added.

"Otto, I love you," Isabel said rather abruptly.

"Are you ready for the third kiss, then?"

She answered by turning her face toward his.

Even as they embraced, he took the ring from his pocket and slipped it on her finger. "This ring is too small," he said, "to stand for all it represents."

"A ring that large couldn't be made," she said.

"Yes, love is always greater than the jewelry that symbolizes it." Then Otto thought of saying "I love you," but he didn't.

Isabel also thought of saying it, but she didn't.

The moment seemed too sacred to voice their souls' best promises.

The sun dipped lower now, and the abundant

shade this created helped to cool the furnacelike effect of the August day.

Isabel and Otto celebrated their love in silence.

Together they pushed with their feet off the porch's floor and set the swing into a bold new glide. Gravity moved them back, and the swing creaked a little, then leaped forward as if it were the *Spirit of St. Louis* lifting high into thin air. Suddenly they were airborne, flying over the heavy weather they once feared. On, on they soared! Far below them they could see the town, the church, the dairy farm. But up where they flew there was only sun and blue sky and a glittering orbit to tomorrow.